Run to the

Reigning Hearts – Book One

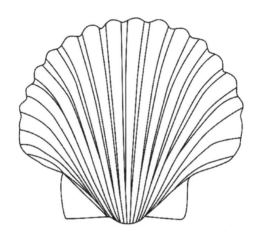

KG FLETCHER

love wishes
KG Fletcher

RUN TO THE SEA

FAIR WARNING: This book contains scenes of detailed intimacy and liberal use of profanity. It is intended for readers 18+

Run to the Sea
Reigning Hearts – Book One

Run to the Sea is part of the
~Reigning Hearts ~ collection.
Each book in the series is STANDALONE
* Run to the Sea
* Stars Fall From the Sky
* A Sun So Bright

For a complete list of KG's books visit:
www.kgfletcherauthor.com

Edited by Vicky Burkholder
Cover art by Eva Talia Designs

DEDICATION

For Hutch
My sensitive artist.

KG FLETCHER

CHAPTER ONE

"Em, Order up!"

Emeline Fischer sucked in her stomach and stood on her tiptoes to get around her pregnant coworker and friend who jotted down a breakfast order at a booth along the wall. Quickly, she bee-lined it to the food counter.

"Extra crispy bacon, right Harold?" she asked, taking a swift breath.

"Yes, ma'am. Just like you asked. Would I ever let you down, Emmy?" One side of Harold's mouth jacked up into a stupid grin revealing a few gaps where he was missing teeth.

"Thank you," she sing-songed while batting her eyelashes at the middle-aged cook.

The Shack offered the best and cheapest breakfast in the tiny beach town, always packed from sun-up through the lunchtime hour. At two o'clock sharp, the place closed. It was a breakfast-brunch-lunch kind of place, the dinner time crowd having to explore other options at the trendier restaurants along Main Street.

Emeline quickly grabbed the rest of her order and placed it on a large, round tray which she hoisted above her shoulder. Crossing the checkered linoleum to the corner booth by the window, she eyed the other tables along the way to make sure her customers were happy. Classic country music played on the old jukebox near the front door, and she couldn't help but hum along to an old Patsy Cline tune.

"Here we are. Ham and cheese omelet, side of grits, white toast with grape jelly and a side of extra-crispy bacon. Can I get you anything else?" She efficiently displayed each dish in front of the lone customer.

The frumpy old woman grinned at the food spread before her and gleefully nodded. She was a familiar face in the area and always ordered the exact same breakfast when she came in. The oversized muumuus she wore were colorful, and her gray hair parted into braids looked like two snakes slithering over her shoulders. Her looks were deceiving, and Emeline knew her to be a retired college professor—a snowbird who came every winter to escape the dreaded cold up north. As the days started to get longer and the weather warmer, Emeline knew it was almost time for all the snowbirds to migrate back to their homes up north, the summer tourist season quickly approaching.

"A little more coffee would be good. Oh, and I used all the little sugar packets, can you bring me some more of those too?"

Emeline always took good care of her customers and was often generously tipped. Even though Miss Muumuu didn't shower the staff with compliments, she made up for it by leaving several greenbacks laid out on the table after she finished.

"You got it."

The diner was bustling during the peak breakfast hour. The sounds of tinkling glasses, forks and knives sliding across greasy plates and happy customers conversing over their morning meals were odd but familiar comforts to her anxious mind. It was part of the soundtrack to her life. Being a local in the Sandersville Beach area came with its ups and downs. Mainly, the other locals seemed to know her family history which made it hard to stay under the radar in the sleepy beach town, especially when she was working. The sideways glances and pitiful looks of sorrow were a constant reminder of her past. She had moved on, so why couldn't they?

In addition to her diner job, she held other odd jobs including being an indie painter and a part-time hostess at one of the Pineapple Grove art galleries where various artists from all over the southeast had showings. The fancy nighttime parties were always a massive hit with artisans showing off their latest collections. All she had to do was stand pretty in her black cocktail dress by the front doors and greet the happy tourists who came for the free champagne and a glimpse of something special. She was excited about the latest artist coming in town—a petite California woman famous for her extraordinary beach paintings. Emeline knew the show coming up would be a success. Being a hostess at a gallery was a consolation prize of sorts, her own dreams of being a successful, full-time artist put on the back burner due to her family circumstance. Ever the eternal optimist, she forged ahead and knew her time would come—someday.

After dropping off a handful of sugar packets to the snowbird, refilling coffee mugs up and down the aisle and helping her co-workers clear off a couple of tables, Emeline paused behind the diner counter and took a sip of water out of a bottle with her name marked on it.

"Hey."

Emeline turned and smiled at her close friend, Ginger. The white apron around her pregnant belly was barely tied in a knot at the small of her back, and her ankles appeared swollen in her white sneakers.

"How are you holding up, Mama? You need a break?"

Ginger vigorously nodded. "I gotta pee again. Do you mind? Fran just sat a guy in my section. I'm afraid if I don't pee before I get over there, I'm gonna leave a puddle on the floor."

"Go," Emeline chuckled, gently pushing her in the direction of the bathroom. Tucking a russet curl over her ear that had come out of her ponytail, she glanced at Ginger's section. The breakfast crowd was in full throttle, the place packed. Pulling a pad of paper and a pencil out of her apron pocket, she approached the table in the middle of the boisterous crowd ready to greet the man who sat alone.

"Hey there. Are you ready to order or do you need a few more minutes?" Speaking a little louder than usual over the noise of people and country music, she tilted her head to try to make eye contact with the man. When he looked up, her heart free fell into her stomach.

"*Cappy?*" It was instant recognition, the handsome face of Thomas Capshaw forever branded in her mind. His dark hair was neatly combed back from his masculine, chiseled face and his full lips parted slightly as he stood and towered over her.

His expression changed from furrowed brow to joyous recognition in a millisecond, his mouth turned up into a gigantic grin when he realized who she was. "Emeline Fischer."

"Oh, my god! It is you!" Excitedly, she threw her pad and pencil onto the table and opened her arms wide, practically lunging at her childhood friend. Their hug was awkward, his body stiff and unyielding. When she pulled back, they gazed at each other, the sounds in the room nothing but white noise in her ears. Right away she noticed his eyes. They were the same, intoxicating blue eyes she had spent countless days and nights staring into as they navigated their childhood and teenage summers together. But they were different too. The bright blue was gone, clouded over with a gray sadness causing her heart to fill with concern. She realized she was still squeezing one of his hard biceps and immediately pulled back and apologized.

"I'm sorry," she chuckled, embarrassed. Using her fingertips, she couldn't help it and lightly ran them down his forearm a second more as if making sure he was real. Not sure how to overcome the uncomfortable moment, she deliberately clasped her hands in front of her apron. "I thought I might see you at your grandfather's funeral—"

"You went?" he interrupted, a look of anguish crossing his handsome features.

Emeline raised her eyebrows in astonishment. "Of course. He was very dear to me. To all of us around here. You know that."

Briefly, Thomas hung his head, and she heard him sigh. When he looked back up, his lips were turned up in a tight smile. "Yes, he was." His voice was low and even-tempered. "I'm sorry I couldn't make it until now. It's been...rough."

Emeline nodded and compassionately reached out to touch his arm again. "I'm so sorry for your loss, Cappy. I know you must miss him. He was a great man."

Before he could reply, Ginger interrupted. "Hey there. Thanks, Em. I can take over now."

Thomas and Emeline continued to stare at each other, the tension evident between them.

"Geez, is everything all right?" Ginger absentmindedly started to rub her belly as she looked back and forth between the two of them.

Emeline startled out of her gaze and cleared her throat. "Yes...yes. Ginger, this here is an old friend of mine. You knew his grandfather, Lawrence Capshaw?" Her voice lilted at the end of the sentence, the name of his grandfather unrecoverable from her lips letting the cat out of the bag. Immediately, she felt remorse knowing that was the last thing Thomas would want to talk about with a complete stranger.

"Larry of Cap Cottage?" She gasped and turned to him with a look of empathy across her face. "Oh, Lord. He is missed, darlin'. I'm deeply sorry for your loss." Ginger's pregnancy hormones must have been raging, and she started to fret over him like a Southern mama bear. "Let me get you some strong coffee, darlin' while you take a quick peek at the menu. I promise, I'll get you some breakfast ordered as fast as I can."

As Thomas numbly sat in his chair, Em caught his eye once more before he turned his attention to Ginger. Gone was the warmth he had generously shared all those summers so long ago. In its place was a cold, shell of a man. Backing up slowly, Emeline cleared her throat again and waved, gaining his attention. "I'll see ya around, Cappy." He responded with a quick nod, too caught up in Ginger's mothering.

Emeline pursed her lips together and quickly darted into the kitchen. With her back against the swinging door, she tightly closed her eyes thwarting off warm tears that threatened to surface. The loss of Lawrence Capshaw was huge in the small community. She recalled the little church in the middle of town that overflowed with locals who had come to pay their respects, Emeline among the crowd. In hopes that Cappy was there, she had scanned the room several times and was sorely disappointed to see only his mother sitting with some of the late Mr. Capshaw's closest friends. It concerned her that Thomas didn't even show up for the funeral. Wild horses couldn't have kept the Thomas she knew from it. He was not the same boy she had spent summers with eons ago.

Over the years she had yearned for that moment when she would see Thomas Capshaw again. The mere sight of him in the restaurant brought back all kinds of memories, her emotions teetering on edge. His grandfather had been a staple in the small, artistic community, and when she would often see him out and about with his wide-brimmed hat and camera over his shoulder, her heart would quicken, as if Cappy might be right behind him. But he wasn't.

He seemed to have vanished forever, his grandfather tight-lipped with vague disapproval regarding his

7

grandson's "big city living". His abrupt departure from the family had caused a lot of grief, especially for Lawrence Capshaw. The old man seemed to have aged faster from not having his only grandson in his life anymore. Never in a million years could Em imagine Cappy living in New York working as an architect. Whatever happened was a mystery.

"Em? You feelin' okay?" With a spatula in his hand, grease splattered on his apron, and concern etched across his leathery face, the friendly cook stared back at her.

"Um…actually, no, I'm not, Harold. Do you mind if I leave? All three of my tables are finished. They just need to check out. Ginger and Fran can keep the tips."

"You look like you saw a ghost. You're white as a hard-boiled egg."

She nodded. "Yeah. I'll…I'll see ya later, Harold." Quickly, she untied her apron and threw it on a shelf, grabbing her small purse in the process. Her long ponytail flew behind her like the tails of a kite as she ran down the stairs of the back of the restaurant. She couldn't get out of there fast enough.

CHAPTER TWO

Thomas didn't realize how hungry he was until Ginger set a huge plate of food in front of him. With wide eyes, he looked at the steaming omelet cooked to perfection and his mouth watered.

"You need anything else?" Ginger asked, refreshing his coffee.

"No. This looks great. Thanks." She nodded, and he watched her wobble slowly toward the kitchen holding the small of her back.

Taking his time, he savored each bite of food, thankful for the uninterrupted meal. Most of the restaurant had cleared out by this time, and he wondered when Emeline might come back out on the floor, so they could continue their conversation. Earlier, her presence had caught him off guard, and he felt terrible for being a standoffish jerk. He wasn't expecting to see a grown-up version of Emeline.

A long time ago, they were the best of friends, joined at the hip every summer through their teens. The last summer he spent with her was especially memorable as they frolicked in the ocean and incessantly teased each other, fighting off their exploding teenage hormones. Thomas often wondered whatever became of her, surprised that she was a waitress. Back in the day, she was obsessed with her art, determined to get out of the one-stoplight-beach-town and make it on her own.

Not only was he surprised to find her as a waitress, but he was also floored at how gorgeous she was. Gone were the chubby cheeks and short bangs of her tomboy youth. Grown-up Emeline was tall and lithe, her mature eyes the color of polished amber. Her beauty and easy-going nature were a striking contrast to his ex-girlfriend, Fiona, who still wasn't convinced they were taking a break from their relationship. The rich socialite and his boss's only daughter could have been a beautiful woman, but her ever-present "resting-bitch-face" and matching attitude knocked her out of contention by most standards. In the early days of his career, Thomas was a workaholic and rarely socialized, the loneliness becoming almost unbearable. He latched on to Fiona who filled a massive void in his life at the time. When he learned the news about his grandfather's death, Fiona was indifferent and never offered a hint of sympathy for what he was going through. He decided to distance himself and take a break from their relationship for fear of coming completely unglued. Truth be told, he was thrilled to be thousands of miles away—glad to have some distance from his chaotic life in the Big Apple even though the circumstances for which he arrived were heartbreaking.

Thomas wished he could sit down and have a lengthy conversation with Emeline after all these years. Not only did he want to know about her life, but out of everyone in town, he knew he could trust her and ask about his grandfather's last days. If she had gone to the funeral, she must have known he was dying. Maybe she spent some time with him during those last months of his life? If so, he probably talked about what a disappointment his only grandson was to the family.

Thomas sighed. It was his fault he hadn't kept in touch with Emeline. While he attended college, she sent numerous letters to him—letters he never answered, determined to move on from his pipe dreams on the coast and make something of himself. He couldn't blame her for not wanting to come back out and talk to him.

The pace of life in Sandersville Beach was staggeringly slow compared to New York. He forgot what it felt like to take his time—to enjoy a simple omelet for a change. When he finished his breakfast, Thomas leaned his elbows on the Formica table top and savored the last of his coffee as he looked around and noticed the various art, including photographs, on the walls. The small, vibrant town was an artist's Mecca and many of the businesses often decorated with the wares of the locals. He'd spent every summer of his childhood until he went off to college living with Lawrence "Pop" Capshaw on the sandy beaches of the Atlantic coastline in Florida, many of those seasons some of the best years of his life. His pop was a father figure to him after losing his own dad when he was just a toddler. Those memorable summers were when he came of age and discovered his natural artistic abilities. It certainly helped that Lawrence Capshaw was a renowned photographer, famous for his nature photos and popular calendars.

A lover of the environment, the late Mr. Capshaw found decades of inspiration while combing unspoiled beaches, saltwater lagoons, inter-coastal waterways, and protected wildlife refuges. Thomas fondly recalled his impressionable teenage years biking for miles on eco-friendly adventures with Pop and enjoying the small-town charm of Main Street. They would take weekly gallery strolls, shop at the vintage market, and get treats from the quaint cafés. Adirondack chairs painted with tropical scenes that lined the brick sidewalk through town beckoned them to sit and chat for hours, and the camaraderie continued during frequent outdoor festivals from farmers' markets to craft fairs.

Pop was a staple in the community, especially in the up-and-coming arts district, Pineapple Grove, where he opened a small photo gallery. Artists in the district, including his grandfather, often invited folks into their space to watch them work and talk about their inspiration. The vivid memories were at the forefront of his mind, a kaleidoscope of color and warmth and love—an innocent time growing up as his grandfather cultivated Thomas's talent, urging him to always follow his heart.

The memories quickly faded, and he could feel the hollowness creep in again, the massive emptiness he felt a reminder of his loss. How was he going to continue without his grandfather's tenacious insistence that he was meant for something more? Why did he not make amends before he died? He knew the answer to that. Because he was a kept man—a poser—a beck-and-call guy—a fucking cabana-boy to the wealthy Merrill family in New York City who owned the architectural firm where he worked.

He took a deep breath and shook his head slowly, determined not to dwell on the life he had put on hold. Scanning the artwork on the walls of the diner, his eyes landed on an abstract oil painting in shades of blue. The swirls in the image were somehow familiar and reminded him of the ocean—azure waves churning under a stormy sky. For some reason, the artwork drew him in immediately.

When Ginger came back by with his check, he inquired. "Are the pieces of art for sale in here?"

Her smile was instant on her glowing face. "They sure are. The prices and artist names are on little tags in the righthand corner. You see something you like?"

"Maybe." He stood and handed the woman a twenty-dollar bill. "Keep the change."

Ginger inhaled sharply, Thomas's generous tip causing her cheeks to flush. His meal only cost five dollars. "Thank you!"

He offered her a rare smile. "You're welcome."

Ginger started to gather his dirty dishes as he moseyed to the far wall to get a better look at the 25 by 32-inch painting nestled in a pine frame. When he lifted the small tag to check out the artist, he exhaled a quick breath and began to chuckle in surprise. No wonder he was captivated. The painting belonged to Emeline.

"*Run to the Sea*," he whispered, reading the title of the painting below her name. He stepped back and let his eyes roam the piece, a sure calm settling over him. The images conveyed a certain maturity and emotion he wasn't used to. Unlike the fantasy-filled mermaid and still-life paintings of her youth, this piece had depth and remarkable power. He wanted to know what inspired the now grownup Emeline to create such a beautiful piece of art.

"Do you like it? It's one of Em's best." Ginger was standing next to him with her hand on her hip.

"How long has it been for sale?"

Ginger sighed. "Not long. She switches out her paintings weekly hoping to get an offer one of these days. I swear, her paintings don't belong in a diner. They should be displayed in a gallery where people can look at them up close and see how beautiful they really are. She spends hours working on them. I've been telling her all these years to have her own showing at the gallery instead of schlepping champagne for the tourists. Maybe someday, huh?"

"I want it," Thomas suddenly vocalized. He turned and determinedly looked the waitress in the eye. "Can you go get Emeline and let her know I want to buy it?"

Shaking her head, Ginger stuttered, "Uh...she's already gone for the day."

Careful not to show his disappointment, Thomas pressed on. "Well, who can I pay to take it with me now?"

Ginger's mouth blossomed into an ear-splitting grin. "You can pay the cashier. And don't worry, all the money will go directly to Em. She's going to be thrilled!"

"Cool." He watched Ginger bite her lower lip and shift her pregnant body as if she wanted to say something else.

"You know, she'll be at the Arts Center later tonight helping out with the seven o'clock drawing class. Maybe you should stop by and...catch up? You could also pay her in person."

***

That view.

Thomas stood on the weathered top stair of his

grandfather's beach home and stared at the vast ocean beyond the natural bulging sand dunes that stretched out to eternity. It had been a very long time since he laid eyes on this part of the world. The salty wind whipped at his hair as the loud roar of the Atlantic Ocean seemed to applaud his arrival with an encore of the crashing waves against the surf. He shifted his gaze to a couple who walked along the frothy shoreline, and the trail of footprints they left in the sand under the cloudy sky entranced him. His mood was overcast like the sky, and the steady sounds of the ocean and wind lulled him into a hypnotic state. His fingers twitched, and he had an overwhelming urge to scoop up large handfuls of sand and watch the grains fall between his fingers. His life was in free fall since his grandfather's passing, the hole in his heart as deep as the ocean water reflecting in his sad eyes.

When his mother called him with some unexpected news about his grandfather's will, he flew commercial from New York to Ft. Lauderdale and rented a car, driving the remaining two hours to the sleepy beach town. Thankful for the large block of time to think, the hours slowly ticked by as he cruised I-95 and reminisced about his grandfather's paradise in Sandersville Beach. It was a hidden gem nestled on the east coast of Florida, and nicknamed Florida's "Little Village by the Sea." His grandfather spent his last days in the well-preserved historic beachfront cottage, finally succumbing to the hideous colon cancer that killed him. Thomas shook his head in despair. Just like the sands in an hourglass, he had run out of time.

Not wanting to face the community that rallied around Lawrence in his final days, Thomas made the bold decision to forgo the funeral, much to his mother's displeasure. She begged him to be there, but Thomas thought the onslaught of familiar faces and memories would surely destroy him.

When Thomas first arrived at his grandfather's beach cottage the night before, he vaguely knew what to expect when he entered the 1914 bungalow. His mom had cleaned out most of Pop's belongings in the last month since his passing, including his photo equipment and a few antiques. What was left was an eclectic sort of mismatched furniture pieces covered in white sheets and unexpected bits of treasure on empty shelves. A hospital bed that hadn't been picked up yet had also been left behind in the master suite—a painful reminder of Lawrence Capshaw's final days.

The small, 1350 square foot space had been thoroughly cleaned, and someone had made up the guestroom bed with new sheets that had been washed in lavender scented soap. Thomas hung his clothes in the small closet and put his toothbrush in a glass on the porcelain sink ledge of the private bathroom. The ocean view from his bedroom was the same as in his youth, the sights and sounds of his young adult life haunting him in a fitful night's sleep. When he finally got up, the only thing on his mind was food. The Shack was a hop-skip-and-a-jump from the tiny back road parallel to this part of the beach, and it took him no time to drive there that morning. The unexpected pleasure of running into Emeline and buying one of her paintings had lifted his spirits.

Thomas ran his hand across the horizontal dark wood siding of the living room and was pleasantly surprised when he felt a nail head already sticking out of the wall. When he hung the hook of Emeline's painting on it, he stepped back with satisfaction. It looked like it always belonged in the room. Keeping the French doors that led out to the weathered deck with a panoramic view of the ocean opened wide, the salty, cool breeze wafted in, and the subtle sounds of low tide added to the mystery of the painting as he admired it from afar. He was anxious to talk to Em again and probe her about her work. The painting he bought was magnificent, and he wanted to see more from her collection. At least she stayed true to her calling, her incredible talent on full display. There was something to be said for following your heart and your passion. Knowing she had stayed the course left Thomas deeply contented.

The boards of the walkway leading down to the beach were warm from the sun. When Thomas stepped barefoot onto the cool sand, he lingered for a moment, wiggling his toes into the grainy path. The wind swirled around his hair, and he squinted, looking up into the sky dotted with clouds. His chest rose as he inhaled the seaweed scent of the water, the sound of the waves thunderous in his ears. He half expected to see his grandfather bringing up the rear, wearing his token hat and carrying his expensive camera.

"You never know when Mother Nature might present a beauty of a shot!" Lawrence Capshaw's voice echoed in Thomas's memory.

The overwhelming grief gripped at his heart, and he clamped his eyes shut, willing the tears away. He needed closure. But how? How could he ever forgive himself for not being there for his grandfather during his final days— for not having the decency to pay his last respects at the funeral? When he first learned of the terminal diagnosis, he should have gone with his gut and left on the first flight out. Too little too late, all because of an overwhelming feeling of obligation to a spoiled rich girl and her father's firm. Cursing into the wind, he shook his head and fisted his hands at his sides, willing himself not to break down.

Slowly walking along the shoreline, he calmed down and marveled at the shimmering rays of sunlight that peeked through the clouds onto the ocean's surface. Lawrence Capshaw had an eye for catching the natural light at the perfect angle in his famous photographs. He took thousands of clicks until he was satisfied he got the best shot. Thomas stopped and stood at the edge of water, letting the frigid froth cover his toes. With his hands on his hips, he lifted his head toward the sky, allowing a passing sunbeam to penetrate his pale skin.

"I'm sorry," he whispered into the sea breeze, his voice cracking with pent up emotion, hoping his grandfather could hear him wherever he might be. His jaw clenched, and more tears leaked out of the corners of his tightly shut eyes. "I'm sorry for not being there for you. Show me how to make it up to you. Show me, Pop. Please."

Thomas opened his eyes and squatted near the water's edge, palming the sand with trembling hands. Scanning the same horizon his grandfather had looked at countless times during his eighty-two years on earth, he could make out a shrimp boat in the distance, and a lone paddle boarder in a wetsuit rowing his way north toward the pier. The noon sun seemed to turn brighter as it glimmered through the patchy clouds, and he shadowed his eyes with his hand over his brow when his gaze caught movement in the water closer to the beach. He focused on the shimmer for several seconds before the familiar sight of dorsal fins popped out of the ocean, causing him to grin from ear to ear. As the fins disappeared beneath the surface, a small chuckle escaped his lips. He stood and wiped the sand off his hands on his pleated pants. Many of Lawrence Capshaw's award-winning photos were of dolphins. Thomas took this as a sign.

"I know you hear me, Pop," he sighed. The undulating,

slow movement of the pod was mesmerizing, the beauty at that moment one he would never forget. The angst he had felt earlier vanished and the weight of the world lifted from his shoulders.

There was no one else on the beach, the open stretch of sand in front of the cottage deserted except for Thomas. But he wasn't alone. He could feel his grandfather's presence as if he were standing right next to him on the shore. As the tears started again, a small ember of hope ignited in his core. Knowing deep down that his grandfather was for him and not against him, Thomas sighed and gripped the back of his neck in exhaustion before he trudged back toward the beach cottage along the wooden walkway. The saw grass swayed back and forth in the breeze as the humble residence came into view. He paused and took in the sight of the cottage that had been Pop's home for nearly fifty years. After the funeral, his mom called him in New York to let him know what was left to him in the will. Thomas was bewildered—Lawrence Capshaw had willed him something more precious than anything he could think of. He left him Cap Cottage.

At first, Thomas was overwhelmed and thrilled. Knowing his grandfather had thought about him in his last days brought unfathomable comfort during his grief. Cap Cottage had always felt like home to him. For Pop to leave it to him was an act of love and forgiveness—he could feel it down to his toes.

Standing tall on the weathered deck among the achingly acquainted landscape with the strong scent of the ocean swirling around him, Thomas finally took a breath. With his head held high, he turned one last time toward the water and swiped the stray tears from his face. It was time to pay his respects to his grandfather who had always known what was best for him.

Cap Cottage was where he belonged. Why did it take him years of stubbornness and ultimately his grandfather's death for him finally to realize it?

CHAPTER THREE

Emeline yanked off her sweats, shimmied out of her tight tee-shirt and bra and slipped off her flip-flops before she grabbed the thin robe off the back of the utility closet door hook and shrugged it on. She was barely on time, and bits of paint were still splattered on the back of her hands she hadn't cleaned all the way off in her haste to get to the Arts Center for the evening drawing class. After her shift at the diner that morning, she poured herself into a new painting back at her apartment for the rest of the day, determined to get her mind off Thomas. When a long line of deep throttled motorcycles sped past the front of her building, she looked up to check the time and left in a rush, so she wouldn't be late to her gig, the splatters of paint a reminder of her haste.

Every single instructor at the Arts Center from the pottery ladies and stained-glass crew, to the photographers and painters knew Emeline and often hired her for various odd jobs during their scheduled classes. The extra money was decent and being around the other artists allowed her to network.

Tonight, she was a semi-nude model for the Advanced

Drawing class, something she had done numerous times in the past. Her job was to sit perfectly still in a specific position and allow the students to study her body and sketch. Thankful to keep her panties on, she was never completely nude. But there were times when she was bare-chested, including tonight, as the teacher had indicated in an earlier email.

As she stood in the back of the room with her arms crossed in front of the robe, she watched students meander in and chat among themselves as they waited for the instructor to show up. Emeline sighed and leaned against the wall, her thoughts reverting to Thomas Capshaw. She felt terrible for leaving the diner so abruptly but needed space to get a grip on how she was feeling. All the years wondering where he was and what he was doing, and he just showed up at the diner—*poof!*

She wondered how long he was staying and if he might come back for breakfast before he left. Perhaps she could stop by Cap Cottage and talk to him one-on-one and find out what his life was like in New York. As closed off as Thomas was that morning, he was still as handsome as ever, his strong jawline and full lips reminding her of blissful afternoons spent on the beach that last summer they were together…

"Hey Emeline, good to see you. You ready?"

Emeline was startled out of her daydream and stood upright with surprise. "Yes. Hey, Meaghan. Show me what you want tonight."

The middle-aged female teacher walked toward the front of the room as Emeline trailed behind. When they got to the staging area, she hopped up on a wooden platform, much like a stage and situated in a way where all the students had good sight lines. As she sat on the soft blanket that had been laid out for her, she listened to instructions, tucking her legs under her and shifting her body until she was comfortable. Meaghan lightly touched her arms and showed her where to place them before she stood back and eyed the final position. A few more adjustments were made until she was satisfied.

"Take your hair out of your ponytail and muss it up a bit, like you just got out of bed."

Emeline did as she was told and allowed the woman to gently move a long strand to trail over her clavicle to her breasts.

"There we are. Now if you could open the robe and let it fall off your shoulders exposing your chest, I think we have it."

"Where do you want me to focus?" she asked, shifting the robe and revealing her chest for all to see. Modesty had never been an issue, and she wasn't fazed, used to being half-naked in a bathing suit most of her life living near the ocean.

"You can look down at your hands. No smiling today. Deep thoughts, okay?"

"Got it."

Emeline listened to Meaghan give her students final directions before the woman walked to the back of the room and turned on a sound machine. Soft mood music wafted into the space, giving a bit of ambiance while allowing the students to concentrate on their drawing for the next forty-five minutes.

Sighing, Emeline allowed herself to relax, and peered at her paint-splattered hands nestled in her lap. After running away from Thomas at the diner, she spent the better part of the day immersed in a new painting, experimenting with different shades of green on a large canvas in her tiny rental apartment. Painting was her passion and her escape when she was stressed, especially as she tried to free her mind of her handsome childhood friend.

"Cappy," as she lovingly called him all those years growing up together, was a mature man now, and good lord, was he ever handsome. Flashbacks of their last summer together filtered through her mind like a long roll of film in one of Lawrence Capshaw's black canisters. Back then, the boy she knew was happy and energetic, a big tease making her laugh until the muscles in her stomach ached. They were inseparable, crisscrossing the beach on bicycles, their tanned skin always peppered with a layer of salt and sand.

Emeline spent a lot of time at Cap Cottage during those days, especially when her mother married husband number three during a time when she was an impressionable teen. Unlike the first two marriages, including the one to her biological father who was deceased, this stepfather was volatile and abusive. He couldn't handle the highs and lows of her mother's bipolar disorder, the two of them fighting on many a night. Emeline would often crawl out her bedroom window and escape the violent shouting matches into the warm bed of Thomas Capshaw. The first night she snuck in through an open window and slipped under his covers, he wrapped his arms protectively around her and made a vow to keep her safe.

"You can stay here every night if you want to, Em. I promise I'll always look after you."

Cappy's voice echoed in her mind as she thought about his arms around her. A shift had happened in their relationship that night long ago. They were no longer two kids having fun in the summer—they were two young adults relying on each other for friendship, love, and protection.

He must have told his grandfather about her volatile stepfather because the next morning she awoke to Lawrence Capshaw offering his famous cinnamon toast while gently probing her with innocent questions about her home life. Emeline didn't give too much away, the very thought of her stepfather's repercussions a hideous thought. With a little reassurance, she let them know she was okay and that she knew exactly where to go if things got out of hand. That was the last summer she spent at Cap Cottage, the lingering images of a happy, overly protective Thomas embedded in her memory.

As Emeline's right foot started to fall asleep, she gently shifted and kept her contemplation lowered. The room was cold, and her nipples were in a full salute. When she heard Meaghan speaking quietly with someone in the back of the room, she curiously lifted her gaze to peer through her lashes to see what was going on. Her breath caught in her throat as she watched Thomas confidently amble to the front of the room to an empty easel. Looking away, she tried to keep her chest from rising and falling heavily, the nearness of Cappy causing her to reel with self-consciousness. Blinking her eyes rapidly, she fought the urge to cover herself with her arms, determined not to let him see her coming undone in all her exposed glory. As close as they were that last summer together, he had never seen her bare breasts, except maybe a glimpse that one time when a random wave hit her, and she lost her bathing suit top.

"Hey, Em," he whispered, taking a seat, acting nonchalant.

Through gritted teeth, trying not to move her lips, she quietly spoke. "What are you doing here?" A glimpse of his smile made her hold her breath as he settled behind the drawing board with a bit of charcoal in between his fingers. Not saying a word, his gaze seemed to focus directly on her, and his brow creased as he studied her and began to sketch, acting like he'd been coming to this class for months. Several seconds passed before he finally spoke.

"I heard you'd be here, and I wanted to talk to you." The low timbre of his voice hummed as he peeked behind the easel every so often.

"You could have waited until after the class," she replied, aware that his eyes traveled down her exposed chest as he ever-so-slightly licked his top lip with his tongue. His fingers weren't even on her, and she swore she could feel the heat from his imaginary touch.

"I like to draw," he said, matter-of-factly, his lips curling up into a devious smile. This was the Cappy she knew and loved. He was back.

"You're dead meat," she mumbled, concentrating on the green flecks of paint on the tops of her hands while stifling a grin. He chuckled and continued to use his hands in broad strokes creating something on the paper in front of him. Emeline's left foot started to twitch with nerves, and she wondered how much longer she could last before Meaghan called time.

"I forgot how cute you are when you're mad," Cappy

teased.

Emeline growled which caused him to laugh out loud. The minutes ticked by and she caught hints of him concentrating on his art, the look of contentment on his face adorable. The bright blue of his azure eyes had returned, and he seemed more relaxed. His hair was messy and hung over one eyebrow reminding her of afternoons during those summers long ago when he would sketch. Happy to sit back and draw the world around him, he always seemed to have a pad of paper and a pencil on him, or he would grab a napkin or a receipt at a restaurant. Many times, he would sketch her—while she was tanning on the beach, reading a book on the deck, or sipping coffee in the local café with him. She often wondered what became of those sketch pads and would give anything to flip through one now and reminisce about those carefree days of youth.

Finally, the music stopped, and Meaghan came up to the front of the classroom and placed her hand on Emeline's shoulder letting her know time was up. Quickly, she pulled the robe to cover her exposed chest and tightened it at her waist. Shoving her long hair over her ear, she paused to look at Cappy who was staring back at her with a look of pleasure on his face. Swinging her bare legs over the platform, she clutched the robe at the lapels and listened to the instructor move on to the critique phase of the class.

The handful of students, including Cappy, shuffled from easel to easel and listened to their instructor talk about proportion and dynamics, the group critiquing one another's work. Emeline listened intently, curious to see the image Cappy captured on his easel. Glancing at the group at the back of the room, she hopped off the stage and took a few steps to where she was right in front of his artwork. Her eyes grew large, the image in front of her, breathtaking. He was a gifted, talented artist back in the day, often drawing silly cartoons of the two of them and their shenanigans on Sandersville Beach. But this…this was different. He had captured something truly beautiful in her that made her blush.

Finally, the group made their way to Cappy's easel and gathered around. Meaghan seemed surprised and gushed over the drawing.

"See class? Here is an example of an artist who has a strong ability to understand and render the human body. Just look at this subtle stroke of her breast, the softness he has created around the curve. The elongated neck isn't too overdone and proportionate with the rest of her body, the detail in the lips and hair extraordinary. Very nice work!"

Several students lingered and studied the drawing up close, a few of them asking Cappy questions. Emeline excused herself to go change as the cluster chatted about his piece. He seemed subdued and almost embarrassed but took the compliments like a champ, acting like he had been a part of the artist community for years. Modeling fees were collected from each student and by the time Emeline returned fully clothed, Meaghan handed her an envelope with her payment inside.

"Is there a place nearby where I could buy you a drink?" Cappy asked, coming up beside her as he rolled his drawing into a tight tube and wrapped it with a rubber band.

Emeline smiled shyly over her shoulder as they exited the classroom, giddy he wanted to spend more time with her. "Sure. There's a pub a couple of blocks from here."

"Cool. I owe you a drink after the way I behaved this morning." He palmed the small of her back as he led her out the doorway, the heat from his hand instant.

"Oh?" Not wanting to come off as snippy with a wise-ass reply, she feigned innocence, delighted he was about to explain his earlier behavior.

"Yeah, I was kind of in shock when I saw you, Em."

They strolled along the brick sidewalk lined with tall palm trees wrapped in twinkle lights that lit up the night sky. A live band could be heard coming from a corner bar and the laughter of diners resonated from a nearby open-air restaurant. Even in the off-season, the small beach town seemed to come alive at night in the walkable downtown district. A cool ocean breeze blew Emeline's hair over her shoulders, and she shivered.

"Are you cold? Here, take my jacket."

"That's okay, we're almost there."

Cappy insisted and pulled off his light windbreaker, carefully hanging it over her shoulders. Thankful for the warmth, she didn't protest and enjoyed the lingering aroma of his citrusy cologne on the fabric. When they approached the big, oak doors of the Brew Dog Pub, Emeline stopped, turned, and poignantly looked up at him.

"Just so you know, I was shocked to see you too." A heavy sigh emitted from his body and he nodded. "And furthermore, yours was the best drawing in the class tonight, no doubt."

A subtle smile crossed his handsome features among the twinkle lights as he rested the rolled-up drawing on his shoulder looking like a baseball player about to approach the mound. "Hmm," he peered at her with one eyebrow raised playfully. "I bet you say that to all your childhood friends." With his free hand, he started to hoist the large door open.

Emeline hesitated before the words left her mouth. "Only the ones I missed the most."

CHAPTER FOUR

The Brew Dog Pub swarmed with thirsty artists, locals, and what appeared to be a few tourists as Thomas followed Emeline inside. He watched her nod and politely say, "hello" to several people who seemed to know her as they made their way to an empty corner booth in the back.

The sturdy table was a solid piece of oak, and the seats reminded him of old church pews, the hard bench made more comfortable with well-worn cushions in deep shades of red. Sliding in opposite each other, he finally relaxed and set his rolled-up drawing next to him before interlocking his fingers together on top of the varnished tabletop. After seeing his childhood friend in all her bare glory, he was more than ready for a deep dive into her current situation anxious to know more about her life. Before he could utter a word, a cheerful waitress with several colorful tattoos running up and down her arms offered a warm welcome and asked what they wanted to drink.

Thomas couldn't help but watch Emeline lick her lips and confidently order a double tequila on the rocks with extra lime. The mere thought of tequila sent a rush of a memory of the two of them as they sat in the hot sun on the beach, passing a bottle they had swiped from his grandfather's stash back and forth, wasting the day away without a care in the world.

"And you, handsome?"

Thomas blinked several times coming back from the sudden blast of his past and fumbled with the cardboard stock menu.

"I'll have one of your local brews," he replied, pointing to the list. "Whatever your best seller is." He smiled up at the waitress who gave a quick nod and a wink. When he turned his attention to Emeline, she was leaned back and smiling at him with her arms crossed against her chest looking like a young girl holding a secret. "What?" Thomas chuckled.

"Nothing. This. Us, together again after all these years."

"I know, right? How long has it been?" Thankful there was no canned music or piano to spoil their conversation, he stretched his forearms across the scuffed table and leaned closer. The happy hum of chatter sprinkled with sudden squalls of laughter filled the entire bar.

"A very long time."

"You're right. Seems like yesterday we were running around in our bathing suits, getting into trouble." They both laughed and didn't say anything for a few seconds before he looked around and changed the subject. "This place is great. What was it before?"

"It used to be Sharky's, remember?"

Thomas grinned. "Oh, yea, that's right. We used to bike over here and get…"

"Milkshakes," they said in unison. He couldn't help but notice Emeline's cheeks flush as they both chuckled at the recollection at the same time.

The waitress returned and dropped off their drinks. "Let me know if y'all want any food. I'll be back in a bit to check on ya."

"Thanks," they said in unison again, making Thomas grin and shake his head. He picked up his beer and held it above the table. "Cheers, Emeline."

Picking up her drink, she bit her lower lip slightly before she commented. "What are we toasting to, Cappy?" Her voice was breathy, with a hint of wistfulness floating over the words.

There were so many things he wanted to drink to. Sitting across from his childhood best friend after all these years was one of them. So was his grandfather's generous gift of Cap Cottage or the fact that he was out of New York and away from Fiona. Lost for a moment in the heat of Emeline's deep, whiskey eyes, nostalgia took over, and Thomas couldn't help but recognize her stare that seemed to hold multiple layers and a complex presence. They were the same eyes he had consumed in his youth, and he savored them like a valuable shot of Glenlivet. The low hum of conversation vibrating up and through the floorboards paired with his beautiful, grown-up friend sitting across from him was a heady mixture of warmth and familiarity.

Clearing his throat, he decided to keep his toast light-hearted, and ceremoniously clinked his glass with hers. "To cocktails instead of milkshakes."

A low giggle erupted before she brought the highball glass up to her mouth and took a sip. "We are grownups now, aren't we?" she asked, her lips glossed with moisture, no doubt lingering with the taste of agave.

"We are. How've you been, Em?"

"I've been…good." There was a slight hesitation in her words. "But I want to know about you. How've you been? Why are you here?"

"Now that's a loaded question," he answered, taking a long drink from his glass biding some time. For some reason, he wasn't ready to tell her about his life in New York, including his recent break with Fiona. After he swallowed, he licked his lips, not sure where to start. "Pop left me Cap Cottage."

Emeline's eyes grew wide, and she leaned forward with purpose. "*No way*! That's incredible, Cappy!" As fast as the smile spread across her face, it slowly disappeared. "What are you going to do with it? Is that why you're here? To get it ready to sell?"

Thomas shook his head and raked his fingers through his hair. "To be honest, I don't know. I took some time off to come down here to figure it out."

"How long?" she interrupted, her enthusiasm apparent.

"I don't know. Not only do I have to figure out what

to do with Cap Cottage, but my mom asked me to go through Pop's office and inventory at his photography studio in town. She was pretty overwhelmed when she was here for the funeral, no thanks to me. Come to find out, Pop paid his studio lease a year in advance, so there wasn't a rush to get his stuff out. I guess I'll get started on it and my mom can finish up when she comes back again."

A small crease had formed between Emeline's eyebrows as she listened intently. She mumbled a sort of "mm-hmm" before she looked away. "Is she still in Atlanta?" she asked, fingering her shot glass with downcast eyes.

"Yep. She's close to her sisters and seems happy enough." He watched her shift in her seat.

"If you need any help with anything, I'm available." When she raised her gaze to meet his, a rush of sweet warmth caused his chest to swell. "I mean if you'd even want me to help you?"

Thomas didn't hesitate. He reached across the table and firmly grasped her wrist. "I'd like that Em. You're practically family. I'd like that very much."

The smile that spread across her face was full of joy. They both leaned back and leisurely picked up their drinks. Thomas took a sip just as Em spoke.

"Now that that's settled, tell me all about New York."

Choking on a swallow of beer, he reached for napkins Emeline immediately passed to him from out of a dispenser. "Thanks," he gurgled, not sure what to tell her.

"You all right?"

"Yeah, it just...went down the wrong pipe." The napkin was pressed against his lips as he coughed again and cleared his throat. "New York is crowded and big."

"I'll bet," she agreed. "So, I know you went to college and then ended up in New York as an architect. I thought you wanted to be a sketch artist?"

Thomas sighed and rolled his eyes. "I know. I guess I decided to use my artistic abilities in something that could earn me more money. Architecture turned out to be the thing."

"Do you like your job?" Her eyes were focused on him, the inquisitive look on her face causing her lips to part slightly. She seemed perplexed.

The booth was suddenly uncomfortable, and he moved against the hard seat back.

"Sometimes. Not really. I don't know." Unsure how to answer, he shook his head. "It's a job. It's not really what I thought it would be."

"I know what you mean." Tipping back her glass, she finished off the tequila in one gulp before grabbing the lime and sucking on it. Her facial expression was comical, her lips puckered around the green citrus.

"You want another? I could use one." Thomas followed suit and tipped back his beer, chugging it in three gulps. The waitress acknowledged his raised hand holding up two fingers.

"New York City. I can't even imagine, Cappy. I mean, I've never been out of the state of Florida."

"Well, it's a cool city to visit, but believe me, you wouldn't want to live there."

"Do you have a lot of friends from work you hang out with? Anyone special?" Her head cocked to the side in that demure, girlish way that indicated she was fishing. He didn't want to tell her about Fiona. Not yet. She was the *last* thing he wanted to talk about.

"I have a few friends, but there's really no time for socializing with my workload." *Especially when you're too busy trying to keep the boss's daughter happy*, he thought.

"What about you? Did you end up going to college?"

Emeline puckered her lips to the side and shook her head. "Nah. I had to deal with some stuff involving my mom for a while…"

"Oh, yeah. How is your mother? Is she still married to that creep?" Images of stepfather number three came to mind, the burly tow-truck driver's smile menacing. Thomas hated the guy for scaring Em and her mom with the emotional abuse he heaped on them.

Emeline's chest lifted in a deep intake of air, and she averted her eyes. "Uh…No. Not married anymore."

"Well, that's good." Thomas knew early on that Emeline's mother suffered from bipolar disorder, her only daughter bearing the brunt of it. Even with prescribed meds, her mom had mood swings and would often sleep all day and suffer from insomnia at night. You never knew what you were going to get with Melony Fischer, her mental health condition worsening over the years causing a multitude of problems in her three marriages, especially the last one. No wonder Emeline never wanted to hang out at her house. Dealing with her stepfather and her mom's euphoria or mania was a toss-up.

Their waitress dropped off round two, and Emeline's eyes shimmered as she muttered a polite, "thank you." She stared at her drink and lightly spun the glass between her fingers. "You don't even know the half of it."

"I'm so sorry you've had to go through that. Is she going to be okay?" The thought of Em taking care of her mother all by herself made him remorseful. If he had known, maybe he could have helped her somehow.

Emeline shook her head and brought the drink up to her mouth to take a quick sip. "I don't have to worry about her anymore. She's in a better, safer place."

Thomas let the moment breathe and quietly drank his beer. For her to give up her college dreams and take care of her mother was admirable. Who knows how many other things she sacrificed staying in the sleepy beach town to watch out for her sick mom? He felt guilty for staying away—guilty for distancing himself from his own family all this time. What kind of person was he to deny his friend and his grandfather a final goodbye? His emotions were running rampant, and he had the sudden urge to be near the ocean.

"You wanna get out of here?" he gently asked.

"Yeah," she whispered, before quickly throwing back her drink in one gulp. Thomas couldn't help but laugh out loud when her expression changed as her lips puckered around the second wedge of lime and sucked the life out of it.

CHAPTER FIVE

The full moon cast silver beams on the surface of the calm ocean, illuminating the ripples that spread out from the small waves that came ashore. They were both bathed in the light against a background of inky blackness dotted with speckled stars in the night sky. The air was crisp, and Emeline tucked her chin under the fabric of Thomas's jacket, nuzzling his essence as they strolled along the shoreline. The tequila had given her a pleasant buzz that loosened her tongue, their conversation finally flowing.

Being near Thomas Capshaw again was a dream come true. For years, he was like a brother to her—someone she could count on when things got tough. He was someone she could confide in and trust. The last summer they were together was a turning point in their relationship. She had felt it. They spent more and more time together, their flirting and innocent teasing something she thrived on. And then he was gone.

"Why didn't you come back, Cappy?" The ocean breeze blew her hair back from her face as she stopped in the sand and waited for an answer. One of his hands was shoved deep into his pants pocket, the other holding onto his drawing. When he turned and faced her, she could barely make out his facial expression as his shadowy silhouette loomed in front of her.

"I got busy with school, Em. My mom and Pop were telling me what to do in one ear, and an overzealous college counselor was telling me what I should do in the other. I knew I wanted to make money. Lots of money. The only way I could do that was to go the architectural route."

"But what about your dreams? What about your amazing talent? You were never money-driven when we were growing up…"

"You sound just like my grandfather," he interrupted tersely.

"Well, maybe we saw something special in you that you couldn't see for yourself. I mean, look at that drawing you just did of me in class. Most people I know couldn't do that." Thomas turned away and started to walk again, his broodiness evident. Emeline followed and matched his slow pace.

"I didn't want to let anybody down, especially Pop. If I stayed here and tried to make it as an artist, people would think I was riding on his coattails—"

"Good god, Cappy. *No*, they wouldn't," she interrupted.

Thomas pressed on. "I thought my new career would be something he could be proud of—something he could gloat about with his artist friends without them thinking he had made a path for me."

"He was proud, Cappy."

"*How do you know?*" he shouted as he abruptly stopped, sending a spray of sand over her shoes.

His sudden outburst caused Emeline's eyes to grow large, and she reached out to touch him. "I just know."

"Did you talk to him about me?" His voice was low, barely penetrating the air around them with the sound of the surf so close.

"Yes, of course. We both missed you terribly. Whenever I saw him in town, I always asked about you. You were always the subject of our conversations."

Before she could say another word, Thomas grabbed her hand and trudged through the sand pulling her toward a familiar set of worn, wooden stairs. When he let go, he ran his hand through his hair and paced, obviously out of sorts. Emeline watched with growing concern and drew his jacket tighter around her body.

"I wanted to be there for him…*I did!*" he yelled into the air. Fisting his hands, he nearly crumpled the drawing and threw his head back, gritting his teeth. "We both said things we didn't mean, and now it's too late." When he turned toward her, she could see his eyes welled with tears. "It's too late, Em! *He's gone*, and I never got to say goodbye!"

It wasn't the look of pain on his face or the way he stood and shivered before her in the night air that made her close the distance between them. No, it was the quiver in his voice—the silent words he conveyed letting her know he was broken and needed her at that moment.

Wrapping her arms around him, he lowered his head into the crevice of her neck and sobbed, gripping her tightly in their embrace. The tears came easily for Emeline too, trickling down her cheeks as she quietly consoled him. It pained her to see him like this. She would never understand the rift that happened between him and his grandfather. All she could do was hold on to him and let the torrent of tears soak her skin. She could feel his fists clench, bunching the fabric of his jacket she wore. Running her fingers across the back of his neck, she attempted to calm the silent war that raged within him. The guilt he must have felt was deep and inconsolable. He wept openly, seemingly lost on the shores of his former life. He needed to know she was there for him, that she would do anything to help him get through this.

Pulling back from her, Thomas took in big gulps of air and wiped his face with his sleeves. Emeline sniffled and ran her hand under her nose as she searched his face.

"I'm sorry, Em," he mumbled, trying to gain some composure. "I'm a real shit-show right now…"

"No, you're not. You're human, and you just lost somebody you loved. It's okay to be emotional, Thomas. It's okay to grieve."

With tears clinging to his eyelashes, he nodded, his chest still heaving as he came down from his emotional outburst. He wiped his face a few more times before he spat on the sand and expelled a long breath. "You ready to head back?" There was a hint of embarrassment in his voice as he pointed toward the stairs with the rolled-up drawing.

"I guess so." They started to walk up the weathered boards. "Are you going to be all right tonight? You want me to hang out with you a little longer?" she asked over her shoulder, hoping he might want to spend more time with her.

"I'm really beat. Can I take a rain check?"

"Sure." Not wanting to push her luck, she left it at that.

Tall shadows of the palms crisscrossed the silent streets in the moonlight as they walked in the direction of the Art Center. It was only a few hours earlier that an animated Thomas Capshaw had been in his element sketching her bare likeness. As they approached the glass doors of their destination, Emeline pointed at his drawing, breaking the awkward silence.

"What are you going to do with that?" she asked.

Thomas glanced at the rolled-up paper in his hand before a small smile played upon his lips. "I'm going to keep it. Maybe finish it later."

"Why?" It was a fair question, one she hoped he'd answer.

"Why not? I happen to like the subject matter."

There he was again, the boy she knew and loved, teasing her in that subtle way she remembered from their youth. Thankful for the diversion, she blushed and licked her lips, trying to stifle a smile of her own. "It was good to see you, Cappy. Thanks for the drinks…and the walk on the beach."

"You're welcome, Em. And, uh…thanks for helping me out tonight."

She nodded and offered a sympathetic smile. Standing under the portico of the Arts Center, they eyed each other uncomfortably as if waiting for the other to speak first. "Well, I guess this is goodbye." Boldly, Emeline took a step forward and lightly kissed Thomas on the cheek, palming his warm chest quickly with her hand.

He grabbed her fingers just as she pulled back. "It's not goodbye, Em. It's only goodnight. Can you still come by the studio tomorrow and help?"

His focus on her face was imploring as a surge of happiness swept through her heart.

Responding with a smile, she squeezed his fingertips. "Yes, of course. I told you I'd help you and I will. I've got to be at the diner for the early shift, so it will have to be around noon. Sound good?"

The color had returned to Thomas's pale complexion, and his smile was genuine. "Sounds great." He paused and looked around. "Where's your car? Are you parked out back?"

Emeline giggled and proceeded to walk to a bike rack situated near the side yard. "I'm parked right here." She used her thumb to roll the combination on her lock and clicked it open. Swinging her leg over the bike frame, she shrugged off his jacket and tossed it to him.

"You're kidding me, right? You still ride a bike?"

"What's wrong with riding a bike? It's cheaper than a car, and it's good exercise. Besides, I live right around the corner. I'll be fine." Before she started to peddle, a thought crossed her mind. "Do you need a ride, Cappy? You can sit on the handlebars while I peddle. It'll be just like old times." An image of her teetering on the handlebars of his beach bike came to mind as he often gave her rides around town. She could almost hear the distant echo of their youthful laughter and feel the summer wind whipping through her hair.

"I'm good." His expression was humored. "My rental car is parked right over there." He used the drawing to point to the nearby parking lot.

Her face felt warm with the blush of the memory riding on his handlebars, and she immediately nodded. "I'll see you tomorrow, Cappy."

As she rode by him, he thrust the drawing forward, bopping her on the head. She laughed out loud and could hear his familiar chuckle behind her. Turning her head to catch one last look at him with her hair flying haphazardly around her face, she yelled. "I'm all grown up, Cappy! I can take care of myself now."

He raised the drawing in a final salute, and she flashed him one last smile. Standing up on the pedals, she pumped the bike hard, leaving her childhood friend in the cold shadows.

CHAPTER SIX

Natural light poured into the large studio space of Capshaw Photography highlighting several enlarged photographs positioned on the white walls. Thomas stood in the center of the room trying to keep his heart from bursting through his chest. His deep breaths echoed within the four walls, making him sound like he had just run a marathon. The larger-than-life photographs were well-known snapshots of the late Mr. Capshaw's award-winning work and glimpses into Thomas's former life.

With misty eyes, he slowly walked the perimeter of the room, stopping at each photo to pay his respects. There was the long shot of Atlantic Beach, peppered with tourists and their summertime wares amidst brightly colored umbrellas dotting the landscape. Several dolphin shots, including the famous photo that won him first place in the International Photography Awards, were lined across the far wall of the room. Rolling ocean waves, sea turtles hatching and glimmers of dancing light on the sea at sunrise and sunset completed the collection, all achingly memorable, all taken through the lens of Lawrence Capshaw's magnificent eye.

Thomas exhaled slowly. "Get a grip, man," he mumbled to himself. He was caught off guard with the bevy of emotions he had gone through in the last two days being in Sandersville Beach. His thoughts reverted to his sob-fest the night before in front of Emeline. Sensitive by nature, he was embarrassed but thankful for her unconditional love at the moment. To finally spew his pent-up emotions unabashedly in front of her had been cathartic. He slept like a baby all night, visions of him and Em as children laughing while bike riding across the sweltering beaches of summer. It pained him that he hadn't been in touch with her all these years. She was someone important to him while growing up, and it was unfortunate that he had cast her aside when he went off to college.

Naïve and entirely unprepared for life in the real world, Thomas decided that architecture was going to be his career path. It sounded very adult and professional to him—a career where he could put his artistic abilities to good use. A career in architecture held value, prestige, and a promising future—something his family could be proud of. His mother lamented his choice of schools was too far away from home, and his famous grandfather remained on the fence with a wait-and-see attitude.

Thomas was glad his grandfather never knew the whole truth about his climb up the corporate ladder after college. Working at one of the largest architectural firms in the world turned out to be a bitter source of contention when it came up between them. He gave up his childhood dream of being a sketch artist to pursue money and prestige, desperate to prove to his mother and his grandfather that he could make it on his own. And then he got caught up in a rip-tide of events that sucked the life out of him…

It happened after graduation when Thomas interned at the prestigious New York firm of Merrill-Seagram-Oliver, founded by architect legend, Robert Merrill and where he eventually landed a stable position as an entry-level architect for the first three years of his career. Thomas often wondered how his grandfather knew he wasn't cut out for the ruthless corporate firm full of hierarchy, or the concrete jungle of the city. It seemed like a supernatural stroke of luck that he was trapped in a broken-down elevator at the downtown New York headquarters, and Robert Merrill's only daughter, Fiona, just happened to be on it too. During the hour they were stuck, he shared his bottle of water with her and talked the gregarious woman out of a full-blown panic attack. When word got back to Mr. Merrill what he had done for her, within a week, Thomas became the leader of his first design team. Soon after, he was invited to dinner at the Merrill mansion in Connecticut where Fiona openly flirted with him throughout the evening.

The attention and instantaneous climb up the corporate ladder were intoxicating, the snowball effect pushing the two of them together under the circumstances. Thomas had the career and the boss's daughter. They started to date exclusively, and it seemed like he won the proverbial lottery. But then came the bribes.

If Fiona wasn't happy, her daddy wasn't happy. It was a vicious cycle and one he grew numb to over the past two years. Mr. Merrill would reward Thomas with special treatment if he kept his daughter placated, including expensive meals out, extra days off to spend with her, and the corner office. Recompensed with a high-paying leadership title he did not deserve, the poor guy vying for the position was livid, and the pressure was on. Thomas knew he didn't deserve it but kept playing the "Keep Fiona Happy" game. She was thrilled with his new position and loved to show him off like a prize poodle in front of her rich friends, often boasting about his success. The high paying, high powered position working with his design team and keeping Fiona happy consumed his life. But he kept going, determined to prove to his colleagues, his family, and even himself, he was cut out for it.

After dating for over a year, Fiona started to badger him incessantly about getting married. Married? Marriage had *never* been on his radar and marrying the rich socialite was the last thing on his mind. When he tried to talk to his grandfather about it, Lawrence seemed to put two and two together and expressed his disappointment that he had used her influence to get ahead in his career instead of earning his new position through good old-fashioned hard work. Thomas assured him that wasn't the case and even lied saying he and Fiona were falling in love. What a load of crap!

The last time he ever heard his grandfather's voice, the man had called in a last-ditch effort, telling him point blank that he deserved real love, not prestige—that being a part of the Merrill family was not his destiny. Thomas told him they would have to agree to disagree and even hung up on him. It was something he would regret for the rest of his life.

When Thomas learned of his grandfather's terminal diagnosis, he was in shock and put the devastating news on a shelf, not wanting to face the inevitable—that the larger-than-life hero he grew up with was close to the end. Looking back, the money, the title, and the wealthy girlfriend never fulfilled him with half the joy his grandfather did. He should have been upfront with him. He shouldn't have lied to his own flesh and blood and made amends before it was too late.

Not able to keep up with the demands of his workload in addition to keeping Fiona Merrill happy at the same time left him in a tailspin, and he was completely losing control. Nothing seemed to matter anymore. His grandfather was gone. How in the hell was he going to pack up his life in New York and break it off with this woman once and for all? He never loved her—it was the instant climb up the corporate ladder and the prestige he thought he loved. He knew he was a prick for leading her on all this time, and he needed to put an end to this nonsense with her father.

When he learned he had inherited Cap Cottage, with tears glistening his eyes, he showed Fiona pictures of his childhood summer home and was caught off guard by her wrinkled nose and shaking head as she displayed repugnance when he tried to share fond memories of the place with her. Her whiney voice was maddening as she nagged incessantly wanting nothing to do with it. She even suggested he sell the home and use the money toward an engagement ring. No fucking way. Having put some distance between them was a good thing. It meant he could get a hold on his own life and finally stop the madness.

Determined to do the right thing for the sake of Lawrence Capshaw's legacy, it was easy for Thomas to let Emeline in again. Besides his own mother, it was oddly comforting knowing she was someone he could trust to help him with this transition. There was also something about her presence that made the loneliness that was embedded in his heart not so noticeable.

Thomas inhaled the strong aroma of the nearby ocean mixed with hints of the lingering scent of Old Spice aftershave as he stood in the middle of the photography studio. Lawrence Capshaw was everywhere. The only thing missing was his physical body. Thomas could feel his impression all around him like a summer puff of air tickling his exposed skin. Goosebumps erupted across his arms as he looked around, half expecting to see his grandfather standing across the room grinning back at him. He shivered and clamped his eyes shut for a moment, waiting for the eerie feeling to wear off.

He pulled a ring of keys out of his pocket, unlocked the office door in the back of the building, and flicked on the lights. The cramped office quarters were chock full of stacks of papers, boxes of photos and three-ring binders and carousels filled with slides. No wonder his mother was overwhelmed. A wall of shelves sagged with the weight of old books and magazines, many of which featured the late Mr. Capshaw's best photographs. A simple calendar hung behind a massive desk—a best seller a decade earlier, the beach landscape under the March heading a brilliant picture of sandpipers posed for a millisecond on the shoreline for Lawrence's camera lens to capture. An empty Coke bottle sat on the desk, and Thomas noticed an open roll of wintergreen Lifesavers lying near the old telephone, the paper wrapper curled slightly at the top. Pop loved his hard candy—the lemon drops and Lifesavers a staple in the old man's diet.

Tugging on the pull string of the blinds, Thomas zipped them up, causing dust to stir and float in the beams of sunlight that filtered through the foggy, salt-covered office window. This was going to take some time to go through. The paperwork would be the easy part. It was the photographs he needed to take his time with, the years and years-worth of talented work his grandfather had dedicated his life to. He couldn't possibly throw any of them out, could he? He was glad Emeline would be there soon to help him with the process. Perhaps she would know what to do with it all. The thought of tossing anything in the garbage was unsettling and not something he was willing to do. Surely there were studios in the area or across the region that might want an original piece of the late-great photographer, Lawrence Capshaw?

His cell phone started to vibrate, startling him. When he looked at the screen and saw Fiona's name again, he sent the call straight to voicemail. Her tenacity was impressive, but he wasn't ready to talk to her yet. She had already called twice that morning, her anxious voicemails full of questions. His lack of communication must have set her off because she never called more than once or twice a day. A third phone call before noon wasn't a good sign. He was sure she would give him an earful which was something he was not looking forward to.

"Cappy? You here?"

Shoving the phone into his pocket, his mood perked up at the sound of Emeline's voice, and he couldn't help the lopsided smile that spread across his face as he jogged to the office door. When he came around the corner to the display room, he stopped in his tracks. Emeline stood tall in the middle of the room with a to-go cup in her hand, seemingly transfixed as she admired one of his grandfather's photos with her head tilted to the side.

"Em?"

She turned sharply in his direction, and shook her head. "I'm sorry. I can't help myself. Your grandfather was an amazing artist. How could anyone get tired of looking at these? They're just breathtaking."

Thomas slowly approached her in the center of the room. They stood side by side and admired the wall of pictures.

"He was brilliant," she whispered.

"Mm-hmm." Not wanting to break down again in front of his friend, this was all he could muster.

"I mean, look at the way he captured that image, Cappy? It seems more real than reality. Does that make sense?"

"Perfect sense."

They stood for a few seconds more before Emeline broke the silence. "Here." She held the lidded cup out for him to take. "I brought you some fresh coffee from the diner. Two sugars, right? I thought you could use some with the work we have to do."

"Thanks, Em. You remembered." The small gesture was meaningful, and Thomas made a mental note to do something special for her too.

"Of course, I remembered. We spent thousands of hours at the coffee house down the street. You always ordered the same thing—black coffee with two sugars." She giggled. "I remember you used to sketch on the paper napkins and leave some of them for the wait staff to pick up. God, Cappy, I'll bet you drew a hundred pictures back then in that one space."

Her youthful grin was infectious, and the light in the space highlighted the subtle pink in her cheeks. Her hair was pulled up into a high ponytail with several fly-away pieces coming out, no doubt from riding her bicycle through town. Her oversized hoodie was zipped up all the way, and white athletic shoes peeked out from under her black yoga pants. Even in her comfortable clothes, the grown-up version of Emeline was beautiful.

Thomas laughed. "Those were the days, huh?"

"They sure were."

"Come on. Let me show you what we're up against." They walked to the back office.

Emeline put her hands on her hips and looked around the cluttered room as if assessing what needed to be done first. "What's the game plan? Are you recycling books and magazines? What about all these boxes of photographs and canisters of film?"

He ran his hand through his hair and shook his head. "I don't know. I hate to throw anything away, but I really don't know what to do with it either. My mom asked me to pack up the most important stuff like his financial papers and awards. He was pretty good about labeling things with dates and such."

Emeline nodded. "What if we start putting things in piles, you know, stuff that's obviously trash, things that are recyclable, and items that are already in chronological order?"

Relief swept through him. Now they were getting somewhere. "Great idea. Let's clear out some space along the wall."

Together, they made an empty area and started to clean up the visible trash. Lawrence was old-fashioned and a diehard newspaper enthusiast with stacks of old periodicals scattered here and there throughout the office. Within the first hour alone, they were able to clean out a substantial area of the room just removing old newspapers and magazines. The empty boxes Thomas had brought in were filled in no time with essential papers, numerous trophies and awards, framed photos and even a key to the city. Securing the last box with a strip of thick tape, Thomas announced it was time to take a break.

"We can tackle the larger boxes of photos later. I'll take those two smaller boxes by the door and the one with the red lid to go through tonight at the cottage. Right now, I'm starved. You want to grab a late lunch?"

Emeline tucked her loose hair over her ear. "Sure."

An hour later, Thomas leaned back contentedly in his chair and looked out the window at the Atlantic Ocean. They had landed at a local seafood restaurant that was popular among the tourists because of the location with sweeping beach views from the main dining room. The seafood chowder and side salad hit the spot, as did the easy conversation and company of his female friend. There was a stark contrast between hanging with Emeline and hanging with Fiona. He determined that Em listened to him—really listened and would often have a humorous reply, making him laugh out loud. Everything about her and Sandersville Beach was a breath of fresh air, and he considered himself happy for the first time in ages.

"Did you get enough to eat?" he asked as he watched Emeline wipe her face and push her dishes to the side.

"Yes. That was great. Thank you." Glancing out the window, she picked up her sweet tea and took a sip. "It's starting to get warmer outside. Before you know it, this place will be wall to wall people with all the vacationers coming back into town."

Thomas nodded. "It's weird. Everything about

Sandersville Beach feels the same, you know? But it's incredibly different too."

"I know what you mean." Her amber eyes drew him in like a moth to a warm flame from across the table. His heart started to pound as he looked back at her, unsure of the electricity he was feeling between them. Clearing his throat, he broke his gaze and changed the subject.

"Do you have any upcoming plans for the summer? Any special friends or family coming to visit?" They hadn't talked much about her life, Thomas selfishly taking up most of their time together with his needs and emotional baggage.

"No," she replied briskly. "No plans. Just working."

Resting his arms across the booth, Thomas nodded. "You seem to work a lot. How many jobs do you have?"

Emeline shook her head. "A few. The diner is the most consistent. I work there several times a week. I also work at the main gallery in Pineapple Grove on the weekends. The Arts Center calls me every other week to model for their drawing classes, and I help some of the contractors in the area refinish cabinetry or do demo work when they get slammed."

"Demo work? You mean with a sledgehammer?" He leaned forward with interest and grinned back at her. The thought of Emeline in a hardhat holding a sledgehammer was intriguing.

"Yes. It's kind of fun getting all your aggression out demolishing stuff. You ought to try it."

It suddenly dawned on him that he hadn't paid for her

painting, their effortless conversations over the past twenty-four hours distracting him. Pulling his wallet out of his back pocket, he retrieved a small envelope and pushed it across the table toward her.

"What's this?" she asked, tentatively eyeing what was inside.

Thomas smiled and secretly hoped for a positive reaction. "I bought your painting at the diner yesterday. Didn't you notice it was gone? I meant to pay you for it last night, but kind of got sidetracked."

"You what?" Her head jerked up, and her amber eyes met his. "You didn't have to do that, Cappy. I'm not a charity case."

"What? *No*, that's not it at all. I *love* your painting! I had to have it." He watched her from across the table mull over his comment before a small smile tugged at her lips.

"You really loved it?" she asked quietly.

"*Yes*. It's hanging in the family room at Cap Cottage like it's belonged there for years. I can't believe how far you've come as an artist. I'm really proud of you, Em. My question is, why don't you have your own gallery showing? Believe me, you're good enough."

Emeline swallowed, and her eyes were wide with awe as she listened to his comments.

Before she could answer, Thomas gently broached the subject of her mother again assuming all her hard work was to help pay for her mom's bills, wherever she ended up. "Do all these jobs keep you from following your passion? Are you doing them to help with the cost of your mother's hospitalization?" He watched her look away, as if embarrassed, the moment ruined by his question.

"Uhh, no. It's taken care of."

Thomas furrowed his brow. "What? You mean like Medicaid funding? I don't understand."

"No." Pinching her lips between her fingers, he watched a nervous Emeline stare out the window again in deep thought. Not wanting to push, he waited patiently for an explanation. When she turned and stared at him with laser-beam focus, the words that left her mouth made his jaw drop.

"My mother's dead, Cappy. She and my stepfather are both dead."

CHAPTER SEVEN

"And you didn't tell him the truth? You just told him they were fighting like normal?"

Emeline rolled her eyes and tucked a throw pillow behind her head as she lay on Ginger's L-shaped sofa. Many a night was spent at the McCormick's tiny house when Ginger's husband, Rusty was on call at the local fire department. The home was warm and comfortable, and the meal she just shared with her friend was homemade and delicious. Even though they had just finished eating, Ginger munched on chips from a bag and offered her some to which she shook her head.

"Why wouldn't you tell him, Emmy? He's your oldest friend, and from the stories you've told me, he kind of knew what was going on with your mom when you were growing up together." Ginger carefully lowered her pregnant self onto the sofa while clutching the bag of chips in her hand.

Crossing her socked feet at the ankles, Emeline sighed. "He's going through a lot right now dealing with his grandfather's death. I told him the truth about what happened without worrying him…"

"Without worrying him with the details leading up to the shooting?" she interrupted. "That your stepfather deserved what happened to him after all those years of abusing you and Melony until she couldn't take it anymore? If your mom hadn't come home early that day, god knows what would have happened to you." Ginger nervously shoved a handful of chips into her mouth and munched away.

Emeline sat up and patted her friend on the arm. "Come on, Ginger. You're getting yourself all worked up. Rusty would kill me if I caused you to go into early labor right now. Calm down and enjoy your chips."

Ginger slowed her chewing down and put her hand on her ample belly, rubbing it gently. "If anyone tried to do anything to my baby girl, I'd kill 'em dead too. Your mom had every right to protect you. I'm just so sad that she died in the process." Her brow furrowed making a deep indentation between her eyebrows.

"I know, Mama Bear," she joked, trying to bring some levity into the uncomfortable conversation that had conjured up terrible memories. "Have I told you that I think you're going to be the best mom ever?"

Ginger smiled knowingly. "Less than six weeks to go! Rusty's already put in for the time off so he can help me those first couple of days after we get home from the hospital."

"And I'm going to help you too. Whatever you need."

"I can't believe it's actually happening for me, Emmy.

I'm living my very own happily ever after!"

Thankful that their conversation had steered onto a happier subject, Emeline couldn't help but totally agree. Rusty and Ginger McCormick were the epitome of a happily ever after. The young couple was madly in love, and the home they had created together was amazing. An American flag was always flapping in the breeze above carefully tended rose bushes near the inviting entryway. Rusty had even put up a partial white-picket-fence in front of their tiny lawn with a promise for a full fence once they had saved enough money for a down payment on a bigger home on the outskirts of town. Emeline loved being around them and was often the third-wheel when they hung out at their house or enjoyed a night on the town. Rusty often joked that Em was like a stray cat, friendly when it was dinner or play time until she disappeared for the night.

"*Oh!*" Ginger suddenly vocalized. Tossing the chips onto the side table, she struggled to sit up. "Here, Em! Feel right here. She's kicking!"

Emeline laid her hand across Ginger's belly and held her breath. When she felt a slight bulge from underneath her skin move up and around, her eyes widened, and they looked at each other in awe.

"I felt it! I felt your baby girl! Oh my god, Ginger. That's so cool. Does it hurt?" She had shifted to where she was sitting cross-legged next to her friend with both hands splayed across her pregnant belly.

Ginger laughed. "It's uncomfortable, especially when I'm trying to sleep. But it doesn't really hurt."

The baby moved again, causing the girls to inhale

sharply before giggling out loud.

"It's the miracle of life." The wonder in her voice was apparent. "Hey, you want some homemade chocolate pudding? I just made it this morning."

"Ginger! How can you keep eating like this? You're a bottomless pit!"

Ginger laughed and shook her head. "I know. After being sick for the first two trimesters, I guess I'm making up for it. I'm hungry *all the time*!" She struggled to hoist herself up and motioned with her hands for Emeline to help her. "Come on, girl. Help me up."

Pulling her by the arm, she gripped Ginger's wrist and elbow until she was steady on her feet. "For the record, I've already gained four pounds hanging out with you."

"That's sympathy weight." Ginger waddled to the kitchen area in the open space and opened the fridge. She turned and offered a brilliant, cheeky smile. "Two spoons?"

Emeline put her hands on her hips and shook her head while trying to stifle a grin. "Oh, all right. What're a few pounds when you're supporting a friend?"

Ginger's face glowed. "Exactly."

***

Thomas raked his top teeth over his bottom lip as he sat and stared at Emeline's painting on the wall in front of him. He had changed into comfortable, low-hanging sweats and sipped from a bottle of beer as he contemplated what she had told him earlier about her mother's death. The old fabric of the sofa was itchy in his shirtless state, and he could hear the faint sounds of the ocean just outside the cottage coming through the window seams. Rummaging through his backpack that lay near his feet, he pulled out his laptop and fired it up, using a Wi-Fi hotspot from his phone. The famous Merrill-Seagram-Oliver Architecture logo screen saver lit up his face and made him grimace. Quickly, he used his index finger and scrolled his way through the internet, intent on finding more details about that fateful night.

The Sandersville Crier was as good a place to start as any, the small hometown newspaper archives easy to navigate. Typing in the name, Melony Fischer, he was dumbstruck at the first headline that popped up.

Local Couple Shot and Killed

It happened while he was away at college. While he got an education and was finding his new path in New York hobnobbing with Fiona and her rich friends playing successful architect, Emeline was an orphan dealing with the aftermath of her mother's violent death. But how could he have known? His grandfather never told him, and Thomas ignored all her letters and lost touch with her when he was in school.

The article was vague, only giving a brief synopsis of what had happened. Apparently, Melony fired the handgun at her husband twice before a struggle ensued. When he had the gun in his possession, he fatally shot her in the chest before turning the gun on himself. The article alluded to domestic violence but didn't give any details on what led up to the shooting that crucial day. Earlier, when Thomas pressed Emeline for answers, she shut down and shrugged his questions off with indifference, conveniently blaming everything on her mother's condition and the couple's troubled past.

A slight hunch burgeoned in his belly as if he knew she was keeping something from him. He needed answers and scrolled through several more articles. Reading through them, he learned that alcohol may have been a factor according to the autopsy reports. His memory of Melony was of a reticent, kind woman who was always happy to see him, not a sick woman gunning down her own husband in an alcohol-induced rage.

Thomas scratched his head and continued online public records search for Palm Beach County in hopes for more answers. Several minutes later, when he stumbled upon a court-issued protective order filed a month before the tragic night by Melony Fischer against her husband, Brannon Otis, his blood ran cold. He didn't have to second guess why Melony fired shots. It wasn't because she had a manic, bipolar episode. No. He knew to his core that she fired the gun at Brannon to protect herself and her only daughter.

"*Shit*," he mumbled, fisting his hand at his side. His problems suddenly seemed insignificant compared to Emeline's.

He wanted to call her and confirm his suspicion, but he knew her too well. He'd have to approach the subject gently, otherwise she'd feign innocence at his presumption. Out of habit, he glanced at the antique cuckoo clock on the wall. It was getting late, and he knew he'd see her the next day at his grandfather's studio. His sweet friend promised to continue to help him sort through the boxes of photos they left stacked against the office wall. He would have to come up with a plan on how to coax her into telling him the truth. Putting the laptop away, he decided to get a head start on the enormous task of sifting through boxes by looking through the few he had brought back to Cap Cottage. With no cable TV, now was as good a time as any.

Taking a long pull from his beer, he sighed heavily in an attempt to get Emeline off his mind and flipped off the lid of box one. Sifting through the contents, most of the medium-sized banker's box contained black canisters of film labeled in his grandfather's cursive handwriting. He decided to leave that one as is and moved on to the next. After an hour of scrutinizing random wildlife and beach photos from decades ago, he pushed box number two to the side as well. He made a mental note to reach out to his grandfather's lawyer and ask him if he knew of any schools he could donate to, the hundreds of similar photos overwhelming him.

Easing his tall frame onto the floor, his biceps bulged as he pulled the third box in between his legs. Unlike the first two boxes, this one had a red lid and was unmarked. When he opened it up, he couldn't believe his eyes.

"Pop, what have you done?" he whispered, surprised at the first couple of photos on top.

They were snapshots of him and Emeline sitting on the weathered deck with the ocean in the background, the two of them in mid-conversation. Thomas had his shirt off exposing his rock-hard, post-pubescent body, and Emeline was wearing a neon-green bikini. Her hair was wet, her bangs plastered to her forehead as if they had just been swimming, and her features were young and soft. Thomas squinted as he tried to make out his own facial expression in one of them, but he was turned awkwardly with most of his back facing the camera. He fingered the photo and flipped it over, peering at the date written in his grandfather's fancy cursive writing. The picture was taken during the last summer he was at Cap Cottage, right before he headed off to college.

A small smile crossed his lips as he remembered that summer long ago. While holding the photo in his hand, he peered into the box and was shocked to see a dozen more pictures of him and Emeline together. His brow wrinkled as he pulled a handful out and quickly looked through them like a deck of cards. There were images of them splashing in the ocean, walking along the beach, on their bikes, and cooking dinner. The further he went into the box, the further the years went back. He guessed there were hundreds of snapshots going back to their elementary school days.

"I don't understand," he muttered aloud with a deep frown. Dumping the entire box out onto the wooden floor, he eagerly sifted through the memories of him and Emeline growing up together. The photos were an unforgettable timeline of every summer he spent in Sandersville Beach at Cap Cottage, the memories rushing at him like a strong wave at high tide. And in almost every single photo was his childhood best friend and companion, Emeline Fisher.

With his heart racing, he pilfered through the pile pausing to look at specific snapshots that caught his eye. There were posed shots of them proudly standing in front of gigantic sandcastles or holding ocean treasures in the air like starfish and shells, their young faces freckled from the sun and their smiles beaming from ear to ear. There were random shots when they didn't even know they were being photographed. He paused, holding up a picture of the two of them sitting in worn beach chairs facing the north pier. Emeline had her head on his shoulder, and they were wide-eyed and open-mouthed watching the July fireworks shooting into the sky, the colored light reflecting in their expressions against the backdrop of the night sky. Running his thumb across her face, he bit his lip as his heart surged with yearning. It was a feeling he hadn't felt in a very long time.

Awestruck at his grandfather's beautiful gift spread all over the floor, Thomas started to laugh. He had no idea the infamous Lawrence Capshaw had kept a time capsule of photographs of him and Emeline. How did they not notice him taking all those pictures over the years? Lawrence was never without his camera and often snapped random shots everywhere they went. That the images happened to be so personal was perplexing. Running his tongue across his upper lip, he stood and gripped the back of his neck scanning the floor flooded with his life. Out of the corner of his eye, he caught a glimpse of something tucked under several glossy pictures. He kneeled and reached for it, realizing it was a small, velvet satchel. It seemed out of sorts among the photographs as he fingered it in his hand.

Emptying the contents into his palm, Thomas's eyes widened with revelation and his mouth gaped as he stared at the antique platinum wedding ring that once belonged to his grandmother. Here in his hand was the ring he had been asking for all those months before his grandfather passed—a ring that was legally his. Why in the world was it kept in a box of photos of him and his childhood friend? Could his grandfather have misplaced it and not been man enough to let Thomas know? Why this priceless heirloom wasn't in a safe-deposit box in a secured bank was beyond him. What if he had thrown out all the boxes from his grandfather's office without looking through them? The questions swirled in Thomas's mind as he sat, dumbfounded on the sofa. Holding the diamond up into the air, he reveled in its beauty, the facets of the rock catching the light. His gaze moved past the jewelry to

Emeline's painting on the wall. Leaning his head back on the sofa, he cocked his head lost in the sea of color on the wall while clutching the treasure in his hand.

The questions in his mind continued to swirl haphazardly like the azure colors in the painting. He wondered if the box of photos and the ring were a message-in-a-bottle attempt from his grandfather's grave. Was he trying to tell him something? Whatever it was, it was deep and meaningful, and he knew it was important.

Slipping the ring onto his pinky finger, he reached for his beer and tipped back the remnants as a certain calm swept over him. Since his first day back at Sandersville Beach, he knew he was at a fork in the road. It suddenly became very clear which path he was going to take.

CHAPTER EIGHT

Fiona Merrill was on a rampage. Her Louboutin heels clicked with purpose against the tiled floors in the opulent lobby of her father's firm as she made her way to the elevators without so much as a hello to the security guard on duty. As the elevator slowly took its time climbing up to the top floor, she closed her eyes and managed a few, deep-cleansing breaths. Her carefully appointed world had been rocked with Thomas's news that he might not be coming back.

As the doors opened, Fiona clutched her fur coat tightly in her arms and stuck her nose in the air, the frown on her face semi-permanent.

"Good afternoon Ms. Merrill. Your father is expecting you," the pretty blonde receptionist offered cautiously.

Fiona's eyes were slits as she gave the woman a forced smile. "Thank you." Rushing past the receptionist's tidy desk, she continued down a long, narrow hallway adorned with plaques and professional photographs of some of the firm's top awarded structures. Grasping the large bronze doorknob of her father's office, she forced the door open and sighed.

"Fiona, sweetie," Robert Merrill's arms were open wide, and she shuffled into his embrace. As if sensing her sulky nature, he squeezed her tight. "What's wrong with my princess?"

Fiona had her eyes closed and pouted, clinging to her father. Anxious for his help, he was the only person in the world she ever confided in. "I'm sad, Daddy. Thomas says he may not come back from Florida."

Mr. Merrill patted her on the back before he took the fur from her arms and hung it on a coat rack. He motioned for her to sit in one of two leather Chesterfield chairs by a large window with a magnificent view of Central Park.

"Have you heard from him?" she asked, sitting with her back erect.

"Now, now. Fiona, you know these things take time. He's probably got a lot on his plate taking care of his grandfather's estate and studio."

"I know that. But have you heard from him?" Her hands were twisting in her lap.

"No, I haven't. You know that Thomas took a leave of absence to deal with everything. I don't expect him back for another week or so."

Exasperated, Fiona stood and walked a few steps toward the window. The trees in the park were still bare, the lingering winter cold penetrating her bones. "Can't you make him come back *now*? Doesn't he have an important job to do? What if he doesn't come back at all?" she whispered, her warm breath causing the window to fog.

"Of course, he's coming back. Why wouldn't he? His position here at the firm is important to him. He would never let his team down. And he has a beautiful girlfriend waiting for him at home. Why would you think such a thing?"

Fiona turned to look at her father's weathered expression twisted with concern. With a heavy sigh, she could feel her eyes welling with tears. "Before Thomas left, he broke up with me…"

"What?" Robert interjected.

She nodded. "He said he needed a break and was using this time away to think things over. Daddy, I don't think he's coming back. I've been calling him three times a day for almost two weeks, and he doesn't answer. He won't call me back either. I hate this! I hate it that he doesn't want me anymore." By this time, the waterworks started, and Fiona was crying unabashedly in front of her father. He quickly took a handkerchief out of his expensive suit pocket and handed it to her.

"Fiona," he started gently. "You're not giving the man the space he needs right now. He asked for some time. You're not giving it to him."

"But I want to know what he's doing. I need to know what he's thinking. I miss him, Daddy."

"I know you do. Come here." He held his arms open again, and she nestled in his arms. "Because of you, Thomas Capshaw is living the dream. Do you honestly think he'd give up his career and his girl to settle for less?

Sweetie, you're the best thing that ever happened to him. Don't you forget it."

Fiona managed a weak nod and pulled back wiping her cheeks. The only time she ever showed even a hint of sentiment was around her father when she used her sullenness to get what she wanted. Maybe she had made a grave mistake not placating Thomas and his emotions when he found out his grandfather had died. He had always been a bit on the passionate side, the sensitive artist in him making her roll her eyes more times than not.

"My suggestion to you is to leave the man alone for a few more days. Give him what he asked for—time. Let him miss *you* for a change. You'll see. He'll come around." Her father smiled as if he had all the answers.

Perhaps he was right. Maybe it was time to lay off the phone and give Thomas space. If it meant he might actually start to miss her, it was worth a shot.

***

Emeline took a little extra time getting ready for the evening. She was anxious to show Thomas the featured art show in the Pineapple Grove arts district where she was a hired hostess for the night at one of the galleries. The past two weeks had been a whirlwind of time spent closely together, going through Lawrence Capshaw's office and often having dinner afterward. It seemed like they had picked up right where they left off, the deep feelings of contentment she felt when she was with him, intoxicating. Ever since she was a little girl, she had been enamored by Cappy. As the days passed, he seemed to open up to her more and more, the blue in his eyes brighter with each minute spent together.

Pulling on a light sweater, Emeline checked herself one last time in the long mirror attached to her bedroom door. She ran her hands down her small waist and turned from side to side admiring the gently used black cocktail dress she had only worn a few times to the gallery. Ginger had recently purged her overflowing jewelry box and had given her a handful of flashy costume trinkets. The shiny faux diamond bracelet and silver hoop earrings made her feel classier as she spread another layer of gloss across her lips. She was thankful she wouldn't have to ruin her curls riding her bike to the gig because Thomas still had his rental car and was picking her up any minute. Excitement flushed her cheeks as she scanned her reflection from top to bottom. She had never been this dressed up in front of him before and wondered if he would tease her about it. A soft knocking on the door jolted her back to reality as she grabbed her small purse on the way to answer it.

"*Ta-da!*" she sang, opening the front door wide and posing dramatically with one hand in the air and the other on her hip.

Thomas immediately grinned, his eyes moving up and down her entire body. "Wow, Em. You look—"

"Like what?" she interrupted. "Silly? You're not used to seeing me all glammed up, are ya?" Her cheeks suddenly felt hot, and she nervously tugged on the sweater around her shoulders. Thomas took a step forward, and they were nose to nose. Looking intently at his face, she was wide-eyed as a waft of citrusy cologne curled around her nostrils.

"You've left me...speechless. God, Emmy. You standing there in that dress. You took the breath right out of my lungs. You're beautiful." His voice was low and husky. A surge of heat pooled in her belly as he kissed her lightly on the cheek. "Aren't you going to invite me inside?"

"What? Um, no. We don't have time, Cappy. I have to be there soon." Embarrassment replaced whatever heat had moved through her body, and she pulled on the door, making sure it was locked. Most of the living space in her apartment was a make-shift studio covered in drop cloths splattered with paint. She wasn't ready for him to see the clutter of art supplies and canvases or explain why most of her furniture was stored in the garage below, hopeful that someday she could afford a larger space that could accommodate her art hobby and her living quarters.

Quickly, she grabbed his hand and pulled him excitedly down the narrow staircase. "You're going to love this artist tonight. The gallery has been trying to book her for months!" Thomas opened the passenger door for her, and she slid inside the car. When he was settled in the driver's seat, he looked over at her and smiled.

"I've been looking forward to tonight all week. I have a surprise for you at my grandfather's gallery after the showing. Think you'll be up for it?"

Emeline's chest heaved with pleasure. He had a surprise for her? What could it possibly be? They had finished clearing everything out of the studio and office that morning. The only items left were the display photos still hanging on the walls. Thomas wasn't ready to part with them and had mentioned something about having one last show to honor the late Lawrence Capshaw.

"Definitely up for it," she replied, her smile radiant.

Two hours later, they stood side by side admiring one of the many paintings on display at the fancy gallery showing. Holding a champagne glass between his index finger and thumb, Thomas tilted his head and seemed to take in the large beach scene in front of him. Emeline admired the expensive suit jacket he wore over his button-down shirt and khaki pants.

"What do you think?" Keeping her voice low, she leaned into his shoulder. Earlier, she had performed her due diligence as hostess for the evening, welcoming artists and tourists as they came in and handing out the champagne. She had even gone around the room offering refills to the crowd several times. The conversations were loud, often interrupted with chortles of tipsy laughter. It was your typical Friday night in the Pineapple Grove Arts District in Sandersville Beach. Add to it the incredible paintings and the company of a handsome Capshaw, and she was in heaven.

"I want to know what *you* think," he replied as he put his free hand into his pants pocket.

Emeline smiled up at him through her lashes before she turned her attention to study the large painting in front of her. "Well, this piece is a bit abstract with the bold use of color. I like that."

"Yes, you were always fascinated with color. Me too. It's very Claude Monet with a California twist."

"Exactly," she giggled and pointed to the left corner of the painting. "The use of light is incredible. It's also really cool that she did a series of this same painting at various times of the day, very true to Monet. See the sun here and how it casts the shadows over there? Her observations in the light changes are spot on."

"You're right."

They moved on to another piece, and she watched him tip the champagne glass back, finishing it off.

"Would you like some more?"

"No. I've had plenty."

"I need to start collecting empty glasses and take out the trash. Will you be okay until I get back?"

"Sure. You want some help?" The way he was looking at her made her heart skip a beat.

Emeline shook her head. "No. You need to relax and enjoy. Ms. Duncan is right over there if you want to talk to her. You two might have a few artist-y things in common. I'll take your empty glass for you, sir." Her tone was teasing, and she was thankful he was enjoying the evening as much as she was. The permanent smile on her face couldn't be helped.

He politely bowed and played along as he handed her his empty glass. "Thank you, madam. Come get me when you're done. I still have that surprise waiting for you."

"Okay."

It didn't take long for Emeline to clean up the gallery space, especially knowing Cappy had a surprise waiting for her. A few folks lingered, animatedly chatting away with the California artist as if they were lifelong friends. Fully immersed in the conversation, she watched Cappy from afar. His countenance was a far cry from when she saw him that very first morning at the diner. He had blossomed over the past two weeks being back in Sandersville Beach. The town was magical with its eclectic artists and diehard locals. The ocean held its own enchantment, often calming even the most uptight tourists after a few days. She realized she was hoping against hope that he would decide to stay—to make a go of it as an artist on his own in her hometown.

Thomas caught her eye and smiled. With a raised eyebrow, she humorously looked from left to right before mouthing the word, "me?" and pointing at herself. He chuckled and nodded before quickly saying goodbye to the group and started toward her. Emeline stood up a little straighter and clasped her hands modestly in front of her black dress.

"You ready to head over to another showing?" There was excitement laced in his voice. He must have found more display photos he had put up in his grandfather's gallery space for the special event he was planning. She couldn't wait.

"Yes. Let's go!"

RUN TO THE SEA

CHAPTER NINE

They talked the entire two blocks through town arm in arm as they made their way to Lawrence Capshaw's gallery. Thomas was eager to see Emeline's reaction to his surprise. When they arrived at the front door, he paused and pulled a red bandanna out of his coat pocket. Her expression was cautious as her eyes met his.

"What's that for?"

"Turn around. This is going to be a true surprise. I don't want you to peek, okay?"

She giggled nervously and obediently turned around for him. "Okay?"

The red bandanna was folded in half, and he carefully placed it over her eyes, tying it behind her head. Breathing in a whiff of her flower-scented hair, his hand twitched to get lost in the long curls. Sliding his hand down her arm, he guided her over the threshold. "I'll tell you when."

Emeline nodded excitedly and tightly gripped his hand

as he led her into the large room. He flicked on the lights and couldn't help but grin, taking in the image of what he had created just for her. Leaning into her ear, he inhaled her scent again, his warm exhale causing strands of her hair to float. "On the count of three, lift up the bandanna."

"Okay." Her cheeks were spotted pink as she bit her dewy lip.

"One. Two. Three."

Thomas watched as she tentatively lifted the bandanna from her face. She started to blink rapidly while taking it all in, her eyes scanning the room up and down and all around. Her mouth fell open in what appeared to be awe, and she started to walk forward, pausing a few times paying close attention to the wonder all around her. He didn't dare say a word, allowing her to experience the memories on her own. The anxious thumping of his heart made him breathe heavier as he stood stoic waiting for her first words of appreciation and squeals of delight at what he had done for her. When she finally turned around to face him, her beautiful face was twisted and streaked with tears, and her entire body trembled. His heart fell to his feet.

"Oh, god. *Not* the response I was hoping for. Em, I'm…I'm so sorry. I didn't mean for you to get upset. That was the last thing I wanted to happen." He started toward her, but she put her palm up, stopping him in his tracks.

Her feet were planted in the center of the room where she was surrounded by thin strands of twinkle lights crisscrossing the space, the photographic images of the two of them growing up together attached by clothespins. Thomas was meticulous in his presentation and chose only the most heartfelt moments of the two of them captured by his grandfather's keen eye and lens. His heart ached thinking about what she had gone through with the death of her mother. Knowing he could shine some bright light on sweet memories they shared together in the photos pre-family drama was something he felt strongly about. To see his Emmy smile was his only goal since they reunited. He watched her dab her face with her sweater sleeve before she inched toward him. Taking a step back, he agonized over her flood of tears instead of the sunny smile he anticipated. When she was close enough, he could see the amber in her eyes was warm and moist, the astonishment on her face real. She reached her hands out and clutched his own, her fingers entwining with his. Thomas held his breath.

"This…" she whispered emotionally, choking on the words. "This is the single greatest surprise of my life."

The sigh of relief that emitted from his body was audible as he watched a big, fat tear roll down her cheek. Skimming his thumb across her skin, his hand lingered and cupped her face, anxious for her emotions to settle.

"Cappy, I will never forget this as long as I live." She leaned her cheek against the palm of his hand as she stared up at him. Lost in the swirl of amber and gold in her appreciative gaze, he was surprised when she wrapped her arms around his waist and hugged him tightly, her voice laced with nostalgia. "Where did you find them all?"

Resting his head on top of hers, he closed his eyes, pure elation coursing through his body as he held her in his arms. He didn't want the perfect moment to end. "Pop had them in that box with the red lid, the one I took home. There are hundreds of them, Em."

"Hundreds?"

Pulling back from her, he nodded. "Yes, hundreds. All photos of just you and me."

Pouring over the snapshots of their time together brought him to this full-circle moment. Emeline was his best friend growing up, and he had cast her aside during the transition in his young life from boy to man. Recently learning about her own trauma while he was gone, the guilt overwhelmed him. It was a miracle she was back in his arms, and he had every intention of making up for the years that were lost to them. The time would come for them to have a sit-down, in-depth conversation about what had happened the night her mother was murdered but for now, he was just happy he had brought a little bit of joy back into her world.

Holding her head in his hands, Thomas tenderly kissed her forehead. Her breath hitched as he boldly leaned down and left a trail of feather-light kisses across her cheek before he landed on her lips. Their kiss was tentative at first, and he wasn't sure she would allow him to cross the brink from friendly peck to full-on make-out. But when she moved her body closer and welcomed his prying tongue with her own, he lost it, his appetite for Emeline unleashing like a tropical storm coming ashore. Ravenous for her, he slid his hands down her sides and gripped her tight buttocks, pulling her forward into his growing bulge. The sweet taste of her mouth was ecstasy, and he couldn't get enough. Her small hands tugged at his hair as she pulsed in his arms, their pent-up desire unbridled and passionate among the photos fluttering in their movement under the tiny, romantic lights. Happiness he hadn't felt in ages exploded in his being, and for the first time in years, Thomas finally felt joy of his own.

"Em…" he muttered into her mouth. She groaned with

pleasure, peppering his face with her lips. "Emmy," he chuckled, pulling back slightly to capture her attention.

"Huh?" Her lips appeared fuller as she blinked back at him. "What, Cappy?" Her breathless voice was sexy, and her bedroom eyes lured him in.

"Do you want to go back to Cap Cottage and look at the rest of the photos?" His inner voice screamed at her to say, yes.

Her whiskey eyes glinted in the light and her eyebrow rose. "What do you think?"

Licking his lower lip, he pulled her in for a bear hug and swung her around the room, making her squeal. The moment wasn't lost on him, the thudding of his heart a reminder that he was a hot-blooded man—and she was all woman.

***

The roar of the surf was loud as Thomas reached for her hand and pulled her through the doorway of Cap Cottage into the familiar home, shutting them inside. With the door closed, the ambient noise of the ocean was less apparent, but still reminded Emeline of holding a large shell to her ear, the hollow interior amplified.

"Wow," she muttered, looking around. "It's so…empty."

Only a few pieces of furniture remained in the living space, Thomas's laptop and some papers taking over the old coffee table in front of the patchwork sofa. She breathed in the familiar aroma and smiled. "But it still smells the same."

Thomas tossed his car keys onto the table. "Oh, yeah. Musty seaweed with a hint of sandalwood. I felt the same way when I first got here. I'd forgotten how pungent ocean smells are in this house."

Emeline giggled at his remark before she noticed her painting hanging on the wall. She took a step further and took in the image. Cappy was right—the painting looked like it had always been hanging in that exact spot for years. There was so much meaning behind the piece, and he had no idea just how apropos it was for it to be in his grandfather's house. Maybe one day she could tell him the truth.

"It looks good, doesn't it?"

"Mm-hmm," she hummed.

"I'm curious Em, why did you name the piece, *Run to the Sea?*"

Her expression fell, and she nervously fiddled with the edge of her sweater. "It's a long story we need to have over coffee sometime. Is that okay?" She tentatively looked up into his face, his concerned expression momentary before he replaced it with a warm smile.

"Sure. You want something to drink?" he asked, changing the subject and shrugging off his jacket before hanging it over a kitchen chair. "I've got some cold beers in the fridge. Pop has a few bottles of booze in the pantry if you want to take a look. There might even be a bottle or two of tequila." The way he was standing there, in the faint light of the tiny galley kitchen staring back at her was a déjà vu moment, and she was thankful he didn't ask any more questions. For a second, she was transported back in time as a teen standing in the very same room looking back at her friend. "What does that look mean?" he asked, grinning at her.

Her cheeks felt hot, and she shook her head. "Nothing. It's just…strange, being here. Everything feels the same, and even smells the same, but it's not. Everything has completely changed."

Thomas nodded and crossed the space between them. Pushing her long hair over her shoulder, he smiled. "Everything has changed, Em. For the better." His eyes were soft looking back at her, and she swallowed hard, the next sentence out of his mouth, a revelation.

"My life in New York has been…lonely. I live and work in a city of eight and a half million people, and I've never been lonelier in my whole life. It's my own fault, I know. I should have stayed in touch with the people I was closest to. I mean, I'm back here for half a month, and I'm happier than I've been in a long time, thanks to you."

"Thanks to me?" Could he tell her heart was pounding? Was her dress pulsing to the rhythm of her blood coursing through her veins?

"Yes. Thanks to you." He grasped her hand and led her to the couch where they sat down. "I owe you a million apologies, Emeline…"

"No," she interrupted, shaking her head quickly. His warm fingers were on her chin and made her stop mid-shake.

"Yes, I do. I'm so sorry I never answered your letters. I'm sorry I never called you or came back to visit. You were my best friend, and I let you down. Can you ever forgive me?"

The lump in her throat was large, and she had to blink several times to keep her focus. For years, she begged the universe to bring her best friend back to Sandersville Beach, especially during the tumultuous time when her mother died. Her knees were bruised from praying so hard, and when she never heard from him again, her heart was broken into a million pieces. And now, here they were sitting on his grandfather's old couch with their hands clasped together, the heat from his thigh radiating through her dress. He traced her lips with his index finger causing her to melt into the fabric.

"Of course, I forgive you, Cappy," she said eagerly. "I'm so sorry the circumstances aren't different for you to come back to. But you have to know by now how happy I am that you're here." The look on his face showed relief. "How long are you going to stay?"

His head tilted as he continued to gaze at her, thwarting off a grin. "It depends."

"On what?"

"You."

"On me?" Overcome with confusion, she scowled back at him, hoping he would explain.

"Yes, you. If I stay longer, will you be my best friend again?"

Emeline rolled her eyes with relief and bit her lip to keep from smiling. He was teasing her again. "Of course, silly. We'll always be friends."

"And…what if this reunited friendship came with benefits?" he continued.

"Benefits? Like what?" The acceleration of her heart made her light-headed. The last summer they were together often included hand holding and flirting. She slept right next to him in his bed for many nights. But as close as they were, they had never crossed over into the adult world of intimacy.

"Bike rides, more kissing, coffee talks, make-out sessions… letting me finish that drawing of you I started?" The pupils in his eyes were dark, obscuring his regular cerulean irises.

Looking down at their hands entwined tightly, she squeezed. The very thought of Thomas seeing her half-naked again sent a delicious shiver up her spine.

"Pop left my easel and art supplies in the closet in my old room," he continued. "I was shocked when I opened the door. A couple of boxes of my old sketch pads are in there too. I haven't looked through any of those yet because I wanted to do it with you. Coming back here has been memory-overload."

The excitement in his voice was understandable. Over the years, she had wondered what had become of his numerous sketches and often reminisced about the innocent time in their lives before all the confusion— before his abrupt departure and her mother's death. With newfound determination, she stood up, took off her cardigan sweater and strode confidently to an empty kitchen chair where she tossed it.

"My modeling fee is seventy-five dollars for an hour, and I will require a shot or two of tequila."

Surprised and seemingly delighted, Thomas stared at her with his mouth in the shape of an 'O,' his eyebrows lifted amusingly. She learned from him a long time ago how to throw the teasing right back.

"What? Too much?" Resting one hand on her hip, she gestured her other hand in his direction and spoke with an over-the-top New York mob-boss accent. "Okay… for you, I'll do it for free on one condition." They had always had an easy banter with each other growing up. That it now happened to have adult content made it even more fun.

Thomas slowly stood and moved stealthily toward her like a wild animal about to pounce. When he spoke, his voice was baritone and smooth. "What's the condition?"

She couldn't help herself and raised her hand to touch his mouth with her fingertips. He grabbed it and kissed her palm, never taking his eyes off her.

"Come back for good, Cappy. Please? This is where you belong."

CHAPTER TEN

Thomas scooted the coffee table across the pine floors and out of the way so he could set up his easel in the family room with a direct sight line to the couch. Fluffing the worn throw pillows, he mulled over Emeline's request for him to stay in Sandersville Beach. He had to admit, he had thought about coming back for years but was too full of pride to leave New York with his tail between his legs. Mr. Merrill had entrusted him with his own design team to which he felt a tremendous obligation to stay and make things work with his career. Right up until he broke it off with Fiona, he also felt a sense of duty to make a go of it with her because of what her father had done for him. His career was handed to him on a silver platter, and as much as he hated to admit it, he owed it all to the Merrill family. Any up-and-coming architect in the firm would kill for a chance to be in Thomas's position. But no one besides his grandfather really knew what he had given up for the sake of it.

Fiona was smitten with him from the beginning, and Thomas knew better than anyone that if she wanted something, she usually got it. Mr. Merrill didn't beat around the bush and offered him his own team on one condition—keep Fiona happy. It sounded easy enough, and they did have a few moments over the years of relaxed fun. Fast forward through the ring fiasco and Pop dying and Thomas threw that obligation out the window. A new spirit of longing and determination blossomed within, and he soldiered forward into the unknown. But it wasn't the unknown—it was Sandersville Beach, Cap Cottage, and Emeline Fischer. They were the familiar sights and sounds that beckoned him to recollect his past so he could move forward into his future. What that entailed, he wasn't sure. But he was damn excited to find out.

Rolling up his sleeves, he stood in the middle of the room and waited for Emeline to come out of the bathroom. Through a little more coercing and a promise to think about her request to stay, she finally relented. He gave her one of his button-down-shirts to put on, anxious to finish his drawing. When the creaky door opened, he turned and was stunned by her innocent beauty.

"Okay, mister. Where do you want me?" The bright pink spots on her cheeks were always the first indication she was nervous. That, and her quirky sense of humor falling into that terrible New York accent.

Quickly, he came to her side. "I think you'll be more comfortable on the couch. Just sit in that same position you were in at the class with your feet tucked up under your legs." His fingers gripped her by the elbow as he led her to the furniture. "I'd really like to see your face though. Don't look down. Look over at me."

"Okay," she said, holding the shirt tightly across her chest.

When she had made herself comfortable, Thomas went

behind the easel and smoothed out the paper that had been rolled up, clamping the corners to the edge of the drawing board. Sitting on the edge of a worn stool, he looked around the side and smiled at her. "I'm ready when you are."

Smiling back at him, she nodded, not moving a muscle.

Thomas raised his eyebrows, humored by her nerves. She was delectable. "You can take the shirt off anytime, Em. Pretend you're back in class. Easy-peasy." He watched her chest rise with a deep breath.

"Okay." With her chin tilted upward with purpose, she leisurely shrugged the shirt off her body, revealing her bare chest, acting as if she owned the place. The only thing she kept on was her black lace panties.

Rising from the stool, Thomas came around the easel and adjusted the lamp on the side table, throwing soft light on the faded tan of her skin. He paused and knelt in front of her, gently pulling a long lock of hair forward to where it hung down to the tip of her nipple. Tempted to lean forward and take the erect bud into his mouth, he took a step back.

"Are you too cold?" he asked.

"No. I'm good," she replied, nonplussed. Her eyes were large, and she watched his every move, hardly making a sound.

Licking his lips, his voice was gravelly when he spoke, aware of the slight ember of heat igniting in his groin. "You're so pretty, Em. Thanks for doing this."

Stifling a small smile, she cleared her throat. "Aren't

you forgetting something?"

Looking around the room, he scratched his head.

"Tequila." The look she was giving him was full of desire.

"Oh, shit. *Yes!* Coming right up." Scrambling to the kitchen, he grabbed the bottle and shot glass he had pulled out while setting up the space minutes before. Placing the glass etched with a capital 'C' on the side table, he unscrewed the cap of the expensive liquor and poured her a shot. "Sorry I don't have any lime to go with it."

"I don't mind," she replied. When he held the glass out for her to take, she immediately threw the shot back in one gulp and started to cough. Her gumption was adorable and made him laugh.

"Is one enough? Or do you need another?" Ready to pour her another shot, he could tell she was trying too hard to play it cool in front of him.

"Just pour another and leave it on the table. Not sure I can handle that again without the lime." Her wet lips glistened in the light, and her face was contorted in a grimace.

"Okay," he chuckled. Another shot was poured before he settled back behind the drawing. "Where were we?"

Breathing deeply through his nose, he picked up a piece of charcoal and took in the image of Emeline posing naturally in front of him. The girl had no idea how fucking beautiful she was. The way her long neck curved when she tilted her head to the side was graceful and elegant, reminding him of a Rembrandt portrait. Her lips were the perfect shade of juicy ripe cherries begging to be plucked, and darker edges of a faded bathing suit tan outlined the creaminess of her perky breasts. His artistic talent easily awakened after being dormant for so long with a muse like her, and his fingers twitched to capture her innocent beauty. With long strokes, he added to the bare bones of his drawing filling in sections he hadn't been able to complete during the class. The entire image came into focus as he used the edge of his pinky finger to smear the charcoal in areas to bring a softer tone to the piece.

Her eyes nervously flitted back and forth from him to the floor as he took his time and concentrated on the details of her face. He was lost in the process—the ecstasy of doing what came naturally not lost on him. Since the night he sat down in that art class and put coal to paper, he had awakened a sleeping giant. His tongue poked out as he concentrated on the curve of her mouth and he absent-mindedly licked his own. Thoughts of their earlier kiss came flooding back, and he had to stop for a minute.

He was reveling in the pure joy of sketching Emeline and paused in the new awareness that smacked him across the face. This is what had been missing in his life. This is what made him feel like himself again. For years, he left the easel in the closet, his sketch pads unopened and blank. His career and the boss's daughter overshadowed what had been most important to him. He had come full circle and all those wasted years were behind him now, the prolonged drought, over. That Emeline was his long-lost muse befuddled him, images of the two of them in the hundreds of photographs exploding in his mind. His grandfather had been right all along, the trail of clues he left, an emotional game he was winning.

Thomas looked down at his hand and stared at the piece of charcoal he was rolling in between his fingers, startled by his awakening conscious as he contemplated his next move. When he didn't poke his head around for several minutes, he was surprised by Emeline's presence when she stood right next to him.

"What's wrong?"

Gripping the white dress shirt between her breasts, she stood next to the board with tousled hair, her stare imploring. This girl was drop-dead gorgeous, and his heart palpitated with immense longing. His Adam's apple bobbed in his throat as he swallowed and looked up at her. Without asking permission, he shifted on the stool and tenderly slid his hands through the gaping shirt. Very slowly, he ran his fingers down the soft skin of her waist before pulling her forward with a grunt. When she placed a hand on his shoulder and ran the other through his hair, the shirt slipped, exposing her breasts. His mouth salivated, and he grabbed her by the buttocks, pulling her forward so he could capture one of her pebbled nipples between his lips. She moaned and threw her head back allowing him to tease and kiss her. He lavished her chest with his tongue, his fingertips digging into her ripe behind, compelling her onto his lap. His dick throbbed with want, and when her lips found his, he bored his tongue into the seam of her mouth as if his life depended on it.

They were a flurry of hands and mouths all over each other when Emeline's hair suddenly caught in the wristband of his watch.

"Ouch!" she bellowed, leaning her head forward so he wouldn't yank anymore. A nervous giggled ensued.

Panting, Thomas gently untangled her hair from his wrist with an unrestrained smile on his face. "I'm sorry, Em. Are you okay?" Pushing the pads of his fingers through her hair at the temple, they were nose to nose, both of their chests rising and falling from the impromptu make-out session.

"Yes. I'm fine." Gathering her hair off her neck, she rolled a rubber band off her wrist to tie it back from her face. Thomas was mesmerized watching her and couldn't help but reach his hand out to stroke her supple cheek.

"Stand for me," he requested.

The rumpled dress shirt hung off her as she pushed against his shoulders and he helped her up. Thomas leaned forward and lifted the edges of her panties with his index fingers. He caught a glimpse of her mouth clenched, and she nodded slightly before he rolled the fabric down her legs. She stepped out of them and shrugged off the shirt at the same time.

This beautiful woman stood naked in front of him like an Italian Corcos painting. Thomas slid his hand up her inner thigh and waited for her to open her stance. When his fingers met her hot seam, he inhaled sharply, her wetness taking him by surprise. He gripped her hip with his free hand and gently inserted a finger into her core. Her moan was masked by the rolling waves of his libido coming ashore. The distant pounding of the tide rumbled beneath him as he moved his fingers back and forth, flicking her swollen nub.

"Em, you're fucking amazing." His mind was free falling with what was happening between them, their transition from childhood besties to lovers inevitable. "That's it. You're so close. You're so beautiful," he encouraged.

Writhing beneath his steady hand, the thick wetness

covered his fingers as she moved faster and faster. When her body started to tremble, her voice pitched in a high squeal, and she became rigid, the orgasm paralyzing her in her stance. Thomas felt a rush of warmth between her legs and continued to stroke her, easing her naked body onto his lap and into his embrace. Her sweet breath came out in short bursts on his skin as she clung tightly to his neck.

"Make love to me, Cappy," she whispered in his ear.

Pulling back, he searched her face. There wasn't a hint of trepidation in her gaze. They were about to make things official and cross the line from friends to lovers. Without hesitation, he lifted her off his lap and pulled her by the hand into his childhood bedroom. Turning on the bedside lamp, he hastily started to unbutton his shirt as she helped him.

When she palmed his skin with her hands, she smiled and continued to run her fingertips across the hard planes of his chest. "I can't believe we're about to do this," she whispered with an intimation of wonder in her voice.

"I can't either." He shimmied out of his shirt and pants and tossed them across the room. Standing in front of her in nothing but his briefs, he couldn't help but shiver when her hand slid down his abs and gripped his engorged penis straining against the fabric. "Lay on the bed," he growled, hoping he could keep his orgasm at bay and enjoy their first time together.

Emeline situated on the queen-size layers as he clumsily pulled the bedside table drawer open too fast, causing it to come all the way out and crash to the floor.

"Easy, fella," she teased, her smile radiant.

Fumbling for his wallet and the two condoms inside, he felt like an inexperienced high school kid about to do it for the first time. Clenching a silver packet between his teeth, he crawled onto the bed and straddled her, anxious to thrust his throbbing appendage inside her.

"This probably won't take long, Em. You've got me all worked up. I'm about to come all over myself," he cajoled. Her artist's hands helped him slide the prophylactic on, and his excitement peaked by her slightest touch as he tried to catch his breath. Leaning back one last time, he grabbed his cock and marveled at her wet, shaved opening, teasing her with his scalding tip. "Are you sure about this?"

Without hesitation, Emeline, his childhood best friend, and teenage dream—the woman who brought joy and art back into his life, grabbed him by the dick and took matters into her own hands.

"Shut up, Cappy and fuck me." Her whiskey eyes were on fire as she pulled him into her hot well leaving him completely flabbergasted.

His hips found a steady rhythm, and she joined him as he climbed higher and higher, never taking his eyes off hers. Sweat trickled down his chest and biceps as he leaned back and lifted her long legs over his shoulders.

"Oh, god, Cappy."

"So...fucking...deep," he uttered before the wave of ecstasy crashed over his head sending him headfirst and swirling into the deep end of the ocean.

CHAPTER ELEVEN

A steady rain came ashore in the early morning, the grayness of the sky a dreary reminder of the fickle Florida weather during the changing season. Emeline was cocooned in Thomas's arms, the warmth of his body penetrating her bare skin. Flashbacks of the night before flooded her mind and she couldn't help but smile and snuggle into his embrace a little tighter. His childhood room was arranged the same, reminding her of the many mornings she had awoken in this very bed. Back in the day, they were two best friends sleeping next to each other. Now they were two lovers sleeping in each other's arms. Listening to the rain and the low rumble of thunder, she scanned the room. The walls were bare, the rock star posters and flags from his youth packed away. The windows were still covered in recognizable blinds causing the dull light to creep in way too early.

Being in Cap Cottage felt like a dream. But the delicious ache between her legs reminded her that what transpired the night before was all too real. Emeline wasn't what you would call, "experienced" by any means. Over the years she had only been with two other guys, neither relationship amounting to anything special. As a hormonal teenager, she had always believed Thomas Capshaw would be her first. That it finally happened was a miracle, and she was anxious to figure out their next steps.

Thomas stirred and burrowed his nose into the back of her neck as they spooned. "Mmmm. Good morning, Em," he whispered in a long, contented sigh.

Her smile was immediate. "Good morning, Cappy." His hand slid across her tummy, and he pulled her closer to his thighs.

"Is it raining?" he muttered, seemingly at ease holding her close.

"Mmm-hmm."

They lay in each other's arms and listened to the rain outside competing with the crashing waves in the ocean. Her eyelids grew heavy, and she had a right mind to go back to sleep but was interrupted when Thomas sat up.

"Oh, man," he lamented, running his hand through his bed-head hair.

"What's wrong?" Pulling the sheet across her bare chest, she arose with concern.

"It's late, and I have a meeting with Pop's lawyer."

"When?" The disappointment washed over her in an instant. She wasn't ready to leave his warm bed. She wasn't prepared for him to leave Florida either. Whatever business she had with Mr. Capshaw's lawyer would only speed up his inevitable departure.

"I'm supposed to be there in twenty minutes."

Emeline peered at the clock on the bedside table. It was almost ten-thirty. Thank god she didn't have the breakfast shift at the Shack, or she would have missed it entirely.

"Can you stay? I won't be long. I need to sign off on some papers. I want to cook for you too, so I'll stop by the store on my way back. Sound good?" He was stroking her cheek with the back of his hand, lulling her into a state of submission as she stared at the sensual dark scruff on his face. Cappy wanted her to stay. How could she refuse?

"I can stay."

His immediate smile rivaled glinting sunbeams on the ocean's surface. "Good! I need to get some more protection too. Last night was off the charts."

His light-hearted comment surprised her and instantly caused her belly to pool with heat as she watched him bounce off the side of the bed and slide on some jeans. The bathroom door shut, and she could hear water running briefly before he appeared again and shrugged on a hoodie. He grabbed his wallet before leaning down to kiss her on the lips.

"I'll be back, Em. There's some coffee in the pantry and some fruit in the fridge. I'll get us something special." His blue eyes sparkled in the gray light as he brushed his lips against hers. When he opened the door, he stopped, turned around and pointed his finger at her, mimicking her pitiful mob-boss accent. "Don't you dare leave this place, okay? I ain't finished with you, doll." His brow was raised, and his hair was boyish and unruly.

Emeline giggled with pleasure. "I won't leave. Be careful in the rain."

"I will." He winked and shut the door behind him.

Emeline shifted lazily and lay on her stomach to look out the rain-streaked window with a pillow tucked under her chin. She watched Thomas run to the car with the hoodie over his head and get in. When the taillights disappeared over the hill past the tall saw grass and dunes, she sighed with bliss. The weather made her want to pull the covers over her head and go back to sleep, but she needed to shower. She was also curious to peek at Thomas's drawing starring her as his muse.

Her feet bare, she padded across the cold floors of the cottage into the en suite bathroom. His things were neatly placed on the vanity where she spotted his cologne. Lifting the designer bottle to her nose, she inhaled deeply, allowing the essence of Thomas to infiltrate her system. Curiosity got the better of her, and she carefully opened the old medicine cabinet that was also part of the bathroom mirror. There was nothing out of the ordinary, just a deodorant stick, an extra tube of toothpaste and a pack of disposable razors—the bare essentials for a man who had come back to town for only a week or so.

After a long shower, she wrapped her wet hair in a towel turban and searched his closet for a shirt and a pair of sweatpants, hoping he wouldn't mind. The only thing she had was her black cocktail dress from the gallery showing the night before, which wouldn't do in this cold weather. Finding suitable clothing, his scent lingered in the fabric as she made her way into the family room.

Everything was how they left it from the night before—her panties and the white dress shirt she had worn laying on the floor. She blushed with the memory and walked over to the easel to look at the drawing that started it all. Shaking her head, she sighed. The added details were impressive, and he had captured a side of her that was enchanting. The happiness she felt was legit, and she so hoped this was only the beginning of his journey back into the art world. It's where he belonged.

Picking up the scattered clothing along the way to the galley kitchen, she felt right at home and foraged in the pantry for coffee items and started a pot. As ribbons of black caffeine percolated in the machine, she finger-combed her long hair and stared out at the churning sea among the rainy landscape. The cottage had been her refuge on more than one occasion back in the day. That she was nestled in its warmth awaiting Thomas's return gave her a peculiar sensation. She turned and looked intently at her own painting hanging on the wall and recalled the motivation for the piece. At some point, she would have to tell Thomas—she would have to tell him the truth.

A vibrating sound against wood startled her, and she spotted Thomas's phone lighting up on the coffee table pushed against the wall. He must have forgotten it and was trying to get in touch with her. She hesitated before flipping it over and read the name of the caller.

Fiona.

With a slight frown, she quickly set the phone back down as if it were covered in germs. Who the hell was Fiona? Crossing her arms against her chest, she held her breath until the phone stopped. Maybe Fiona was his assistant or a co-worker trying to reach him? The questions that reeled in her mind were quickly interrupted when she caught a glimpse of the box with the red lid.

"Our photos," she said out loud.

Sitting on the couch, she took the lid off and had to bite her lower lip to keep from grinning like a clown. There were hundreds of photos tucked inside, all images of her and Thomas growing up together. At first, she was mesmerized sorting through them, laughing out loud at the memories and some of the goofy poses and faces they made as kids. And then she became overwhelmed with melancholy, the images of their young lives together innocent and naïve before both of their worlds changed forever. The tears started, and she shook her head, continuing to look at photo after photo, the memories blurred in her hands. How she wished she could go back.

Time stood still, and she didn't hear Thomas come in. He found her sitting among the pictures scattered on the floor, crying. Pulling her into his arms, he rocked her back and forth, comforting her in a way that only he could.

"Emmy, shhh. Why are you crying? Do the pictures make you sad?" His voice was calm and full of empathy.

"I just…I've missed you so much." She pulled back and wiped her eyes with her knuckles. Searching his face, she watched as his head cocked and his lips pulled up into a half smile.

"I've missed you too, Em." Taking the few photos out of her hand, he studied them. A small chuckle erupted. "What an incredible gift Pop left us. We can treasure these forever."

Her heart clenched. *Forever.* That word held so much promise.

"I got us some food. Are you hungry?"

Her stomach perked up with a growl. Wiping her face again, she beamed with happiness, thankful he was back. "Starving."

***

The rain continued to come down harder as Thomas flipped a grilled cheese sandwich in the frying pan on the stove. The scent of Gruyere, white cheddar and parmesan floated in the air among a hint of basil from the soup he had ladled into large mugs. Emeline was sitting at the kitchen table eagerly awaiting the meal he insisted on making and serving her. His heart was light after signing the papers at the lawyer's office. He was the official new owner of Cap Cottage, and he couldn't wait to tell her the news.

"Here you go," he said, setting the perfectly grilled sourdough bread in front of her with the mug of steaming soup. "I remembered it was your favorite growing up. It's the perfect meal for this rainy day."

Her eyes lit up at the sight of the comfort food, and she licked her lips in anticipation. "Cappy… this is so…thoughtful. And it smells heavenly. Thank you."

He smiled back at her. "You're welcome."

One gooey bite later leaving a string of cheese from her mouth to the plate, he watched as her eyes rolled back and her mouth moved slowly as if savoring the expensive cheese. "God, Cappy. I forgot how good this sandwich is. Promise me you'll make me another one later." Her words were muffled by a full mouth.

Thomas chuckled. "I promise I'll make you this sandwich anytime you want."

Her eyes narrowed as she swallowed. "What does that mean?"

Wiping his lips with a napkin, he leaned forward, anxious to tell her the news. "It's official. Cap Cottage is mine now. I signed the papers this morning."

"*Oh my god*! That's amazing! Congratulations," she exclaimed. Her mood shifted from hot to cold in an instant. "You're not going to sell it now, are you?" Crumbs dotted her lower lip as she stared back at him with intensity.

Reaching across the table, he gripped her hand and squeezed. "I'm not selling it, Em. That's for certain. I do have to go back to New York and settle some business before I can really think about being here permanently. But I think that's the goal—"

"To live here permanently?" she interrupted.

His face beamed with excitement. "I think so, Em. It just feels right being back here. I haven't felt this right in a long time."

He watched her close her eyes and take a deep breath before she opened them back up as if relieved. "What about your job? Your career as an architect? Can you still do that from here?"

Thomas pulled his hand back. "I don't think that's possible. But I could do something else. My grandfather's lawyer is looking over the studio lease with me later today. There are a couple more months still paid on it but I'm thinking I might keep it going if I can. I'd like to have one last show to honor Pop's lifelong work."

"Oh, Cappy, that would be so wonderful. The town would be all over that." Emeline nodded in agreement and took another huge bite of sandwich, her excitement contagious.

"If I can sign a new lease, I've also thought about featuring additional artists like the other galleries in Pineapple Grove do." He hesitated, his heart surging with excitement. "I want you to be the first artist I feature at the gallery after Pop's show."

She stopped chewing, her eyes amber colored laser beams staring at him from across the table, utter astonishment visible across her face. "*Me?*"

"Yes. You. You have no idea how much you've helped me since I came back. You're an amazing talent, Emeline." He reached across the table again and grabbed her hand. "It's time for me to help you."

CHAPTER TWELVE

The Shack was quiet, albeit a few locals who sat at the vintage counter with their backs to the window. The rain continued to come down in a drizzle, old man winter refusing to vacate Sandersville Beach to make room for spring. Emeline and Ginger sat at a booth in the corner and rolled silverware that was still warm to the touch from recently being washed.

"Rusty and I missed you last night. I made your favorite—pot roast."

Emeline couldn't quite look her friend in the eye, her face full of chagrin. "I'm sorry. I should have told you I wasn't coming. That was rude of me."

"Were you with him?"

Her nod was slow and intentional, and she kept her mouth shut, not quite ready to give up any details about her weekend.

"He's a handsome boy, Em, I'll give ya that."

A cross between a hum and an "mmmm" left her lips causing her cheeks to catch on fire. If Ginger only knew.

"I'm just sad he doesn't live here. Are y'all gonna keep in touch?"

Emeline placed a roll of silverware on top of the growing pile. "Definitely."

Ginger waited for a beat before she spun her eyes with exasperation. "Dad-gummit Em! You're not telling me anything!" She leaned back in the booth and absent-mindedly rubbed her protruding belly. "Give me something. Did you have dinner together? Did you kiss?"

Feeling mischievous, Emeline replied with one-word answers. "Yes and, uh… yes!"

"Ooooh," Ginger growled.

Emeline's shoulders relaxed as she laughed. "Okay, okay." Looking around the empty space to make sure no one was within earshot, she leaned forward. Ginger followed suit, her eyes wide with anticipation. "We spent the weekend together at Cap Cottage, which he now legally owns…"

Ginger pursed her lips and squealed. "I knew it! I just knew y'all were gonna reconnect! Tell me everything!"

Emeline was relieved to have her friend to confide in about her reunion with Thomas, the girl-talk a perfect rainy-day diversion. Everything was revealed—the photo surprise at his grandfather's gallery, posing half-nude as his muse, kissing, making love, grilled cheese, and the possibility of him living in Sandersville Beach permanently.

"He wants to do a showing of my paintings if he can secure a new lease at his grandfather's studio."

"Oh, Em! That's always been your dream. It's finally coming true!" Ginger happily took a sip of water before her brow knitted with concern as though a thought crossed her mind. "Does he know about what happened? Did you finally tell him?"

Emeline stared at the Formica table top in front of her and shook her head. "I don't know how to tell him," she said quietly.

"Hmmm." Ginger nodded. "But you know you *need* to tell him, right?"

Looking up at her friend, she could feel the weight of her truth settle on her shoulders. "I will before he leaves."

"Leaves? But he just got here. Why is he leaving?"

Emeline shrugged and started rolling silver again. "He has a whole life back in New York, Ginger. He can't just…disappear from that world. His boss deserves notice, and he has an apartment to take care of…"

"But that could take months," Ginger lamented.

With a heavy sigh, Emeline agreed. "What's a few more weeks or months, right?" The look she gave her friend pleaded with her for reassurance.

Ginger stretched her hand across the table and grabbed her wrist mid-roll, her mama-bear coming out in full force. "Sweet girl, if you can get through what you did with your family, you can get through anything."

By mid-afternoon, the rain had stopped, leaving a damp cold and gray sky behind. Emeline shivered and dodged large puddles on her bike as she made her way back to her garage apartment. When she came around the corner, she was stunned to see Thomas sitting in his rental car waiting for her.

"I thought you got off at three?" Looking incredibly handsome in old ripped jeans and a thick jacket, he slammed the car door shut and walked toward her. The scruff on his face was turning into a subtle beard, and she had the sudden urge to stroke his face.

"I did. Ginger got very chatty, and I lost track of time." She parked the bike under the staircase and pulled the heavy, waterproof jacket off her head, thrilled to see him. Catapulting her body into his, she kissed him on the mouth. "Hi."

"Hi," he replied huskily. His blue eyes shimmered, obviously happy to see her. "God, Emmy. Your nose in frozen! Let's get you inside."

Taking her by the hand, he led her up the steep stairs. When they got to the door, Emeline panicked for a split second realizing he had never been inside. Cap Cottage was where they spent most of their time.

"You know my place is more of an art studio than a home, right?" The key was in her hand, but she hadn't unlocked the door. "I mean, I have a bed, but it's not like Cap Cottage."

"Emeline, I don't care what your place looks like. Unlock the door."

Once inside, she flicked on the lights and watched him as he looked around the space with wide eyes. The main living area was huge, the open concept covered in drop cloths, easels, giant canvases and splatters of paint in a rainbow of colors. Along one wall were dozens of paintings—variations of the ocean and sky, and one particular painting that made Thomas laugh out loud.

"I remember when you painted that, Em! You still have it?" He was pointing to a large canvas on the wall. It was a painting she had done while they were still in high school, the subtle blue and pink orb surrounding a mermaid in a purple ocean rising to the surface. Her body was s-shaped mid-swim, and her arms were arched behind her long mermaid hair flowing past her butt.

Emeline dropped her keys in a basket on a small table by the door and shrugged off her jacket. "Of course, I kept it. That painting is very sentimental to me."

He nodded, grinning from ear to ear as he looked around the place.

"Well, what do you think? This is home."

"You live here?" he asked with a you've-got-to-be-kidding tone.

Laughing, she replied with a hint of pride in her voice, "Yes, I live here. There's a bedroom and bathroom in the back. Most of my furniture is in the garage underneath us. I use this space to create. It's my very own art studio."

Thomas had his hands on his hips taking it all in. "I'm so impressed that you didn't give up like I did."

"You   didn't   give   up,   Cappy.   You   just

got…sidetracked."

"Ha! Yeah, sidetracked. If that's what you want to call it." He moved forward and studied the large canvas she was currently working on. "There is so much beautiful art in this room, I don't even know where to begin."

Emeline could feel butterflies in her tummy as immense pleasure filtered through her body. To be admired by an artist as talented as Thomas Capshaw was a dream.

He turned to her with a knowing smile. "Mark my word, you're gonna sell out of all these, Em. Even your famous mermaid painting if you wanted to." They both laughed. "They're amazing. Really." As he continued to study her artwork, he spoke the next sentence over his shoulder. "By the way, you never told me about the piece I bought, *Run to the Sea*?"

Her heart stopped, and her face paled. She had tried to keep her truth from him for as long as she could. When she didn't answer right away, he turned to look at her.

"What is it?" Concern tinged his voice as he crossed the room and took her hand. "Tell me, Emmy."

Her tongue felt two sizes too big for her mouth, the words stuck in her throat. "I…I need a drink. You want something? I know I have some tequila. There might be a couple of beers rolling around in the fridge too. Whadyasay? It's five o'clock somewhere, right?" She fake-laughed and was blabbering like an idiot. On a mission, she walked to the refrigerator in the tiny kitchen area. Paint brushes and rags littered the countertops, the area turned in to more of a cleaning station than a place to prepare a meal. Lucky for her, she worked at a diner and ate for free.

Quickly, she pulled a beer and lime out of the refrigerator. Popping off the top, she handed a stunned Thomas the beverage before turning her back to him and cutting the lime into wedges. He didn't say a word as she grabbed the bottle of tequila off the top shelf and poured herself a hefty dose into a small glass, throwing it back in two gulps. Pressing the lime into her mouth, she shut her eyes tight, her hands shaking with nerves. When Thomas put his arms around her from behind, she jumped.

"Emeline. Talk to me. Talk to your best friend." His breath was warm on her neck.

Nodding, she tossed the lime into the sink and gripped the counter with both hands, keeping her back to him as she took a deep breath. "After you left, my mother and stepfather's relationship got worse. She called the cops—he called the cops. They fought all the time."

"I remember. That was so wrong of them to do that in front of you."

Her cheeks warmed from the shot of alcohol making its way into her system—liquid courage for her to come clean. The only other people who knew the truth about what really happened were Ginger and her late mother. Thomas was about to be the third.

"Brannon started drinking more and more, especially after a fight with my mom. If I were around, he'd try to pick a fight with me too."

"You mean he would scream at you?"

Her shoulders sagged, and she hung her head. "Yes. It only got physical the last couple of months they were

117

together. Pushing, slapping, getting right in her face…"

"Oh, Em…," he moaned, his grip tightening around her waist. The heat from his body covered her like a warm blanket, but she still shivered, recalling the memory.

"My mother would try to warn me when things were getting out of hand. We had a code phrase. I knew if she used it, I needed to get out of there fast and go to our safe place."

"*Run to the Sea?*"

Turning around slowly in his arms, she nodded. He tucked her hair over her ear, and she noticed his blue eyes had turned gray with sorrow.

"I would run to the pier, or the beach and wait till he passed out or left and then my mom would come and find me. Sometimes the police would be waiting for us, and he would blame it all on my mother's mental health."

"Didn't you tell the police the truth? What was really going on?"

"I couldn't, Cappy. I was scared to death of him, and he told me if I said anything, he would kill her! And then one day, my mother finally had enough, and she somehow talked him into moving out. I don't know how she finally did it. To be on the safe side, she marched herself down to the courthouse and filed a restraining order against him thinking that would surely keep him from ever coming back. He wasn't supposed to come near us." Hot tears started down her face as the dark memories came flooding back. She began to pour another drink, but Thomas stopped her mid-pour.

"Don't," he requested softly, his warm fingers gripping hers around the neck of the bottle. She relented and let go, trying to gather the courage to tell him the rest. "Tell me what happened the night your mother and stepfather died."

The woefulness that overcame her was intense, the recollection of that night haunting her dreams for years. The story spilled out of her like the rain from the sky— tiny droplets at first and then the torrent of an unyielding storm.

On the night of the shooting, Emeline told Thomas it all started innocently enough. She was wearing headphones and listening to music while filling out college applications laying on her bed. It was late, and her mother had the sudden urge to bake cookies—chocolate chip. But she didn't have any eggs.

CHAPTER THIRTEEN

"*I'll be right back,*" Emeline remembered her mother saying. It was a good day when Melony took her meds, the unexpected anticipation of homemade cookies as good as it could get in their small, complicated world. Her stepfather was finally gone, and her mother seemed happy again. From what she had been told, Brannon was staying at a friend's house on the other side of town near the towing company he was part owner of. It was the best-case-scenario knowing he couldn't come within five hundred feet of their home, her mother's small act of gaining a restraining order giving Emeline unrealistic assurance that they were finally safe.

A large hand squeezed the back of her bare thigh as she lay on the bed, startling her.

"*Where's your mama?*" His voice was low and insinuating, the whiskey on his breath obvious. Rolling to her side, she quickly sat up and drew her knees to her chest, not making eye contact. The faint sound of Coldplay music drifted from her headphones she had tossed aside.

"*I asked you a question. Where's your mama?*" When he sat on the edge of the bed, it made a creaking sound, the

120

mattress sinking from his weight. Brannon Otis was a huge man, his strength a plus in the towing business. The man could lift anything, including cars.

"*You're not supposed to be here*," she muttered simply. Her mind was quickly assessing how she could run past him through the open door of her bedroom.

"*Come here. You have something on your face.*"

Her head shook slowly, and he chuckled slightly. "*Come on, Em. You know I'm not gonna hurt you. Fuck the restraining order. I've never laid a hand on you. Now, lean forward, just a bit. Looks like you got some ink on your cheek.*" For once in his life, he was being nice. But she knew better. This was the calm before the storm. "*You must be studying too hard again.*"

With her eyes downcast, she cautiously scooted toward her stepfather hoping her obedience would appease him, hoping that her mother would be there soon to rescue her. The rough skin of his calloused thumb dragged across her cheek, making her wince. When she still wouldn't make eye contact, he grabbed her chin and forced her to look up into his face, his strong hand puckering her lips. His creased forehead and his beady eyes frightened her. Even though she was eighteen and considered a legal adult, she was still just a high school senior and couldn't help but whimper. He stared at her for what seemed like an eternity as if deciding what he was about to do. When he licked his lips, she knew things were about to take a turn for the worse.

Emeline bit him hard on the hand and scrambled to get off the bed. The man bellowed but was too quick and grabbed her by the arm, flinging her like a rag doll back on the mattress.

"*You need to be taught a lesson!*" he screamed, taking off his belt. At first, she thought he was going to beat her, but when he crawled on top of her and forcefully held her hands above her head using his other hand to unzip his pants, she knew...

"*Shit*, Emeline! Did he do it? Did he rape you?"

Thomas was nothing but a blur in front of her, obscured by the tears raining down her face as she told him what happened. As he tenderly wiped her cheeks with his fingertips, she continued her story. "No. No, thank god, my mother came home just in time and must have heard me screaming and crying. The next thing I knew, she was calmly standing at the foot of the bed with a gun pointed right at his head. I didn't even know she had bought a gun. When he started to laugh, she cocked it and said our safe phrase."

"*Run to the Sea?*" Thomas whispered, peering into her face with intensity.

"Yes. She said it and then put one finger over her mouth like she was trying to tell me to be quiet. The look on her face was so strange. I didn't ask questions and got out of there so fast... I had no shoes on. I didn't have my phone. It was dark outside, and I was running down the street toward the beach when I heard the first shot. And then another. There were four shots total. I didn't know what to do. I stopped but knew I couldn't go back. There was no telling what would happen if I went back. I was so scared, Cappy." By this time, she was on memory overload and buried her face into his chest. She felt him hold her tighter, as if he were in protection mode. When she caught her breath, she managed to continue, anxious to finally get it all out.

"I ended up at the beach and paced for over an hour, waiting for my mom to come and find me."

Thomas paused for a beat before he spoke, his face expressing remorse. "But she didn't come."

"No. She didn't."

"What did you do?"

Tucking her hair over her ear again, she shook her head. "I heard the sirens. And then I walked back home. The lights were so bright. I stood and watched with all the other curious neighbors, and the funny thing is, nobody noticed me. My mom and Brannon were carried out one at a time, and I knew they were dead. I knew it was the end." Images of the black body bags came to mind and she shivered.

"I was in total shock, but I finally gathered the courage I needed and told one of the police officers I was Melony Fischer's daughter, and they let me in the house after the ambulances left. I don't remember much after that except they wouldn't let me in my room, and they asked a lot of questions. I *lied* Cappy. I told them I was out taking a walk on the beach when the shootings happened. I didn't tell them he attacked me. I knew without a doubt my mom didn't want anyone to know what Brannon almost did to me—that he almost raped me. My mother said our safe phrase and told to me to be quiet when she put her finger over her mouth. Because of their history calling the station all the time, my mom's mental health and the domestic abuse paper trail and restraining order, it turned out to be an open and shut case. The end."

Emeline could feel her face scrunch with emotion as she tried to hold back the tears. "My mom died protecting me from that monster, even after he was dead."

***

Thomas sat on the lumpy mattress in Emeline's room and waited for her to come out of the shower, his emotions depleted from the story she had just told him. It took her a long time to calm down after telling him everything that happened as he held her trembling body in his arms. When she apologized for not being transparent with him when they first started hanging out again, he assured her he understood and wasn't upset. He suggested she get out of her work clothes and take a long, hot shower and calm down while he waited. There were still so many questions that needed answers as he mulled things over in his mind. The guilt he felt for not being there for her consumed him. The only consolation was, he was with her now.

"Feeling better?" Steam vapors curled slowly into the room when she opened the bathroom door and emerged dressed in a bathrobe.

"Yes," she smiled, towel drying her wet hair. "I don't smell like a French fry anymore." She stood right in front of him, her earlier emotional state replaced with contentment.

"I love French fries."

Her eyebrow rose playfully as she intentionally leaned her thighs against his knees.

Thomas felt his crotch twitch and hesitated to take advantage of the situation after the emotional story she told him earlier. Knowing full well Emeline was naked under the robe, he couldn't help himself and slowly ran his hands over her hips along the fabric. "I want you to know I'm here for you, and I'm not going anywhere."

"You're not?" Her voice was scarce with a come-hither tone, her gleaming amber eyes alive and crackling.

"I want to make it up to you. One day at a time." His fingers dug into her ripe ass, and he pulled her forward. She dropped the towel and let her wet hair hang to one side, tiny droplets hitting his hand.

"One day at a time," she repeated, before boldly untying the robe. She shrugged it off her shoulders and let it drop to the floor where it pooled at her bare feet.

Thomas couldn't help but gasp, his dick straining against his denim. Pulling her by the waist toward him, he kissed her tummy as her hands found their way into his unruly hair. He pulled back when her stomach muscles clenched with a giggle and looked up at her with curiosity, utterly pleased by the amusing sound coming from her mouth.

"Why are you giggling, Emmy?"

"Your whiskers tickle."

"Oh?" He ever-so-slightly ran his chin up and down her skin causing her to guffaw and wiggle in his arms. "I'm growing a beard," he chuckled, thankful the mood was more light-hearted.

"I can tell. It's very Vincent van Gogh," she teased, staring down at him with a suggestive smile. She traced the stubble around his mouth with her index finger, and he puckered his lips, kissing her on the finger mid-circle.

"Do we have time to play?"

Biting her lower lip, she nodded eagerly. "We don't have to be at Ginger's house for dinner for another hour." She kneeled in front of him and unzipped his jeans, his engorged penis springing forward from his commando composition. "Plenty of time."

When her full lips landed on his burning flesh, he exhaled sharply and leaned back on his elbows. Taking him in her mouth, she smothered his skin and sucked in a slow, sexy rhythm he immediately pulsed to. Closing his eyes, he clasped his hands behind his head, leaned back and relaxed concentrating on the exquisite pressure building in his core. He teetered on the edge of orgasm before he sat up with the swiftness of a jungle cat and captured her mouth with his own. They shimmied on the bed, and she took control pulling his jeans off and straddling him.

"There's a condom in the back pocket of my pants," he panted. He watched as she grabbed his jeans and fumbled in the pocket, ripped open the foil packet and efficiently rolled it on. Her body loomed above as he shuddered with desire waiting for her sweet pussy to settle on his aching thickness. Her small hand clenched his hardness, and he reveled in her touch, every thought eliminated from his mind. Arching her back, she slowly eased onto him with copious, wet warmth. Falling headfirst into the pleasure with his jaw clenched and pulse racing, he gripped her hips steadily.

"I'll always have time for you, Emmy." His tone was insistent, and he meant every word.

Her gaze never left his as their desire escalated, full of promise. His mind raced, and blood pounded in his ears when he realized at that moment that what he felt for her was much more than friends with benefits. They were as close as two people could get. The small, gnawing feeling he had pushed away in his youth was suddenly at the forefront of his mind. He shuddered through her in release and fell into waves of inexplicable joy as he cried out his best friend's name at the top of his lungs, finally understanding the hidden meaning in his grandfather's beautiful box of photos—he had always been in love with Emeline.

CHAPTER FOURTEEN

"So, I strapped on the pet-sized oxygen mask and got the kitty inhaling and exhaling again and we transported her just like a patient to the 24-hour vet center."

"Feline resuscitation," Thomas said, shaking his head in amazement. "That's one lucky cat."

Rusty McCormick smiled wide. "Exactly. The owners were so thankful and couldn't believe we went back in to save her. Just one of a few of my favorite fire stories I tell. I can't wait to tell it to my daughter one day." He paused and tenderly placed his hand on Ginger's ample belly. "That, and some of the ocean rescues we've had over the years. I've been pretty lucky in my five years at the station. Nothing too traumatic or terrible to tell you." He eyed Thomas's empty beer bottle. "Hey, man. You want another one?"

"Sure."

The foursome had just finished dinner together, and Thomas was enjoying getting to know Rusty McCormick better. He was one of six full-time emergency response personnel at Station 4 in Sandersville Beach. Dually trained as a Firefighter and Paramedic, he was also part of the Ocean Rescue Team Division. With his handsome good looks and bulging biceps, Thomas wouldn't be surprised if his image was plastered on a wall calendar somewhere dedicated to firemen. His wife, Ginger was obviously enamored by him.

"Rusty, help me up," she requested, struggling to shift her pregnant body to the side of the chair. "I'll get dessert while you get the beer." She gripped Rusty's forearms as he hoisted her up. "I swear, if baby girl doesn't come soon, it's gonna take a forklift to get me up out of a chair." The foursome erupted into laughter.

"You're beautiful, baby. Even eight months pregnant, you're still the most beautiful woman I know."

"Aw, Rusty…" she giggled, leaning her head on his shoulder as he kissed her temple.

Thomas turned to look at Emeline who had her head propped in her hand while leaning her elbow on the table. Her happy gaze shifted to his face, and she turned up her sweet smile a couple of notches just for him.

"You were right. I love them," he said in a low voice.

"I told you."

Thomas was content and reached for her other hand that was resting on her thigh. "They're the perfect pair."

"Yes, they are. They've been together forever," she agreed.

"Kind of like us."

Her eyes shifted to their entwined fingers, and she nodded. "Exactly."

Rusty made his way back into the small dining area carrying a pie in one hand, and two bottled beers by the necks in the other. "Y'all are in luck tonight. Ginger made her famous cherry pie…"

"Alamode!" She interrupted loudly while waddling behind him with a container of vanilla ice cream and a scoop in her hands.

Rusty passed a beer across the table to Thomas. "A little bird told us it was your favorite."

Thomas looked at Emeline, and she nodded. "Guilty. I knew it would be a treat for you. Ginger makes the best pie of anyone I know. You deserve it."

Licking his lips, he watched Ginger cut into the flaky pastry. "Wow, Ginger, you didn't have to go to all this trouble for me."

Waving her free hand in the air, she shook her head. "No trouble at all. I love to bake, and I haven't made this recipe in ages. It's my mama's. She always made it for my daddy's birthday. We're just so glad to finally meet you!"

"See? I told you this was a special occasion." Emeline whispered, poking him in the ribs.

Ginger passed him a plate that held a large slice of pie oozing with cherry goodness and topped with the perfect scoop of ice cream. The three of them watched as he took his first bite. The tart fruit and sweet vanilla hit his tongue in an instant, the flavor a glorious explosion of decadence. He couldn't help but roll his eyes and moan. "Damn, Ginger. That's the best cherry pie I've ever had."

Rusty proudly put his arm across her shoulders as she giggled with elation and held his beer in the air in a salute. "My baby knows how to please," he teased, kissing his wife on her plump cheek before he sat down. Ginger absolutely glowed.

"I detect a Southern accent when you talk. Where are you and your folks from, Ginger?" Thomas asked while taking another huge bite of pie.

Ginger passed another plate of dessert across the table to Emeline. "I grew up in Dixie, Georgia. It's about six miles from Quitman—barely a blip on the map."

"Her daddy sells tractors and farm equipment. Her parents are great. They came down after Hurricane Irma with some equipment and helped clean up downed trees and debris. Super folks." Rusty piped in, taking a swig of beer.

"They're chompin' at the bit to come back after baby girl is born." Ginger handed Rusty a plate and sat down.

"What about you, Thomas? I know from what Emeline has told us you live and work in New York now, but aren't your folks from around here?"

All eyes were on Thomas as he swallowed a mouthful of dessert and wiped his lips with a napkin. "I'm originally from Atlanta. My dad died when I was a toddler, and my mom still resides in Atlanta near her sisters. That's where I was raised."

"But you lived here every summer, in Sandersville Beach, right? With your famous grandfather?" Ginger asked.

Emeline lay her fork on the side of her plate and looked at Thomas with wide eyes while licking her lips. It was as if she sensed this might be a hard conversation for him to continue. With a nod of reassurance to let her know he was okay, he leaned his elbows on the table and proceeded to tell them all about his grandfather and what those summers meant to him. Rusty, Ginger, and Emeline hung on his every word as he told stories of growing up in the shadow of such a famous, beloved man. He even added in some Emmy stories and told them about the box of photographs they had discovered while cleaning out his grandfather's office. There was laughter, and there were even some tears. Ginger's pregnancy hormones erupted when he told them about how he was making plans to have a final showing of his grandfather's most famous photographs to honor him and to make amends for not being at the funeral.

"Oh, god. That's so wonderful," Ginger sobbed. Rusty chuckled as he put his arm around her and tenderly offered his napkin to wipe away her tears.

Thomas could feel Emeline lean her head on his shoulder as the two of them stared across the table at the happy couple, the love and memories saturating the room. Em was right—Rusty and Ginger were the epitome of a happily ever after, their love for each other admirable. If he could be so lucky...

"When are you planning to have the showing?" Rusty asked, taking another pull from his beer.

"Probably when I get back. I have to tie up some loose

ends in New York before I commit to a date." He forlornly took a gulp of his own beer and knew he needed to break the news to Emmy that he was leaving sooner rather than later.

Ginger's face was red from her cry fest. "I'm so sorry, y'all. I cry at the drop of a hat. And I gotta pee again. Oh, Lord, I'm a mess!"

As if on cue, Rusty stood, set his beer down and hoisted his wife up again. "Come on, baby." He turned to Thomas and Emeline. "We'll be right back," he bid humorously.

Thomas nodded and couldn't bring himself to look at Emeline. Staring down at his empty dessert plate, his stomach started to churn as he searched for the right words, knowing his time with her was coming to an end— for now.

"Emmy, I have to leave soon," he whispered quietly.

"I know."

His voice caught in his throat as he turned to look at her. Her amber eyes reflected flickers of candlelight from the table, the warmth of her gaze penetrable. "Em, the thought of leaving you and Sandersville Beach kills me. But you know I have to take care of some things, right?"

"I know," she reiterated. Bringing her hand up to his cheek, she stroked his bearded jawline. "I'll be fine. Don't worry about me. I'm more worried about you."

"Me? Why?"

"When I first saw you at the diner when you came to

133

town, you were so cold and distant. I could tell you were unhappy, and it scared me."

Thomas tensed and remembered the long, miserable travel day that brought him back to Cap Cottage not knowing what he would find. Because of Emeline, he was not the same knocked down man who drove into town that day. Even in their youth, she had always found that spark in him that no one else could see.

"But that's the funny thing about Sandersville Beach," Emeline continued. "It warms you up and thaws you out. I've seen you change in the past couple of weeks, Cappy. You're alive again. You're my Cappy again." The amber color of her irises sparkled like expensive bourbon in crystal glass as her eyes crinkled in a smile. She brought her hands down to his lap and gripped his fingers. "Don't let what's waiting for you in New York freeze you up again. Do what you need to do to get back here. If you have a moment of doubt, just remember how it feels to reconnect with your best friend."

Thomas was surprised when she pulled him forward and hugged him with all her might. Holding her in his arms, he closed his eyes and inhaled her intoxicating essence.

"I'm not going anywhere," she said breathily in his ear. "I'll be right here when you come back."

A knot had formed in his throat, and he nodded, barely able to speak. "I'm counting on it."

CHAPTER FIFTEEN

The yellow cab dropped Thomas off in front of the tall building that housed the architecture firm of Merrill-Seagram-Oliver. Coming directly from LaGuardia Airport, he didn't want to waste precious time giving his notice and traveled straight there without stopping at his apartment. Dressed in slacks, a button-down shirt, and a light jacket, he shivered as a gust of bone-chilling wind hit him straight on as he stepped over a disgusting pile of gray slush shoved up against the curb by passing cars. There were no signs of spring in the New York forecast, a definite nip still lingering in the air. With his rolling luggage in tow, he hoisted his computer bag over his shoulder and entered the large glass doors into the opulent lobby.

The firm had a long history in this building dating back to the 1930s. The art deco lobby was an homage to those earlier days with its intricately tiled floors, gold trimmed columns and tall ceilings illuminated by crystal chandeliers. The great hall held a certain sense of romanticism to which Thomas was fond of. Pausing near a potted plant, he could almost picture Emeline sitting in one of many parlor chairs spread throughout the space sipping on a coffee from the nearby café. Shrugging off the thought, he quickly headed toward a bank of elevators, nodding at the security guard on duty. Once inside, he took a deep breath and pushed the button to the floor where he had left his career on hold a couple of weeks earlier. So much had changed in such a short time and he felt a certain drive again all thanks to his best friend.

The doors dinged open, and he exited into the empty reception area, the large back-lit logo of Merrill-Seagram-Oliver welcoming him in impressive, bold letters. Thankful the admin was away from her desk, he quickly walked down the silent hall to his corner office and unlocked the door while looking at the other open office doors, wondering where everyone was. Parking his luggage close to his desk, he set his computer bag on his office chair and walked over to the floor to ceiling windows to open the blinds. His was a view for a senior team player, not a shmuck carried up the corporate ladder because of the boss's daughter. Thomas shook his head with disgust as he looked out the window at Wall Street below. The faint sounds of car horns and sirens could be heard in the distance, the quintessential city lullaby something he had never gotten used to. The incredible urge to listen to the ocean or Emmy's laugh caused his chest to tighten.

"Mr. Capshaw, I didn't see you come in. How are you?" A pretty twenty-something blonde woman wearing a tight, black pencil skirt and cream-colored blouse stood in the doorframe with file folders in her arms.

"Hey, Ms. Morse. I just got back from the airport."

"Welcome back. Mr. Merrill wanted me to let him know when you arrived. Do you want me to give you a few minutes to get settled before I tell him?"

"Uh, yeah. Sure. That'd be great."

"No problem." She started to close the door.

"Ms. Morse? Where is everyone? I didn't see Taylor or Dean in their offices. Is anyone from my team here?"

Ms. Morse smiled. "It's the first Monday of the month, remember? Everyone's in the conference room enjoying birthday cake."

"Oh. That's right." Thomas recalled the firm generously providing cake from a famous bakery down the street once a month as a sort of social event to celebrate all the birthdays in that month. Most often, he was usually too busy and never partook in the afternoon social break.

"It's chocolate chip Bundt cake this month. You should go grab a piece, especially after your long flight. It's delicious."

Thomas sat behind his desk and looked up at the woman. In the past, he often dismissed her without hesitation. But as she innocently smiled back at him, for the first time, he noticed her blue eyes from behind her tortoise-shell glasses. Ms. Morse had always been kind and accommodating, even on the most stressful of days. Too bad he couldn't say that about himself.

"I just might do that. Thanks, Ms. Morse."

Her smile beamed. "You're welcome."

The door clicked shut, and Thomas pulled his laptop out of his bag. His team had taken care of most matters while he was away, and he did his own due diligence in keeping up with the onslaught of daily emails that filled his inbox. Unfortunately, he was the only one who could tell Mr. Merrill he was leaving the firm. As he read through several correspondences of high importance, he could feel the familiar tension radiate up the back of his neck. Shutting his eyes tight, he slowly breathed in and out the way Emeline had taught him. A small smile graced his lips as he imagined her beautiful face telling him to relax. A knock on the door startled him out of his daydream.

"Come in," he offered, sitting up perfectly straight.

Mr. Merrill entered the office holding a small plate with a piece of cake in his hand. "Thomas! You're back!" The mature man stuck his free hand out, and Thomas quickly stood to shake it.

"Yes, sir. I just flew in. Haven't even been home yet."

"I can see that." The old man mimicked stroking a beard which made Thomas nervously laugh.

"Yeah. I got kind of busy packing up my grandfather's studio and didn't have much free time for shaving. I know facial hair goes against your company policy."

"Oh, I don't care about that right now. I'm glad you're back so I can tell you the good news in person." Mr. Merrill sat in a chair across from him and set the cake on his desk.

"What news is that?" Thomas didn't want to dilly-dally. He wanted to tell Mr. Merrill he was done, the words teetering on the tip of his tongue.

"The Chicago Airport expansion news. You got it, Thomas! Your team won the bid!" The old man's eyes shone brightly.

Thomas couldn't speak, dumbfounded by Mr. Merrill's news. Thomas and his team had replied to a qualification call by the request of the city of Chicago. It was a long shot, the work including demolishing O'Hare's Terminal Two and replacing it with a global concourse and terminal for both domestic and international flights. Their team had been working on this project for more than a year, the likelihood of getting it a toss-up between them and four other reputable American firms. The total costs of the expansion process from design through construction were estimated at approximately 8.7 *billion* dollars. It was the first major overhaul for the airport in twenty-five years and a huge win for the firm. This put Thomas Capshaw on a major playing field with the architectural big-wigs of the world. He was blindsided by this news he didn't see coming.

"Cat got your tongue?" Mr. Merrill teased with an obvious glint in his eye. "Congratulations and a celebration are in order, son. I knew you could do it."

The shock covered him like the heavy slush from the street, and he couldn't breathe. This wasn't supposed to happen. Never in a million years did he think they could win this bid. That it was happening at the worst possible time in his life was an understatement. His workload would increase exponentially, and he'd more than likely have to travel back and forth to Chicago. He suddenly felt like he was being pulled into a riptide, his hand the only thing above water waving frantically at the shore for someone to save him.

"Whe…when did you find out?" Thomas managed to mutter while trying to keep his drowning nerves under wraps. He nervously adjusted the collar of his shirt that suddenly felt too tight.

"Got the call yesterday," the man bellowed. "I knew you were flying in and I wanted to be the first one to tell you before word got out. Chicago leaders are making the official announcement tomorrow. I gotta tell ya, they had nothing but great things to say about you." Mr. Merrill grabbed his plate and took a big bite of cake. "Your team is in the conference room. Why don't you go in there and tell them the good news yourself, now that you're back?" His eyebrow was cocked humorously, and his mouth was full as he grinned from ear to ear looking like the cat who swallowed the canary. Thomas's determination to take a fork in the road was swallowed up with it.

"This is just the beginning, son. I knew I could count on you."

***

Fiona Merrill scrutinized her image in the long mirror with narrowed eyes. The light blue Marchesa tulle gown she wore was embellished with expensive beads, crystals and paillettes and the ankle-length tiered fringe skirt swished when she moved her hips back and forth. It was a show-stopping gown, the slim fit perfect on her small frame reminding her of the roaring twenties. Knowing she was purposefully over-dressed, she slipped on her crystal embellished satin sandals, held her chin high and nodded at her reflection.

"This will cause his head to turn," she muttered under her breath. Her tiny Maltese named Saint was lying on the king-sized bed watching her every move and yipped as if in agreement. A slight smile played on her crimson lips as she flicked her head to look at herself again. Her blonde hair was perfectly flat-ironed in a chic bob framing her angular face. Nervously, she tucked one side over her ear revealing vintage silver earrings and wondered again if she didn't look like she was trying too hard.

Her father had called the night before to let her know Thomas was finally back in town. Why her ex-boyfriend hadn't called to tell her this news himself was beyond frustrating. Keeping her cool, she listened as her father told her about a reception the firm had planned and insisted she be there. Apparently, Thomas had landed a huge deal which would keep him occupied and in New York for years. Thrilled, she decided to take matters into her own hands and called him herself. Much to her surprise, he answered on the first ring.

"Thomas? It's me, Fiona."

"Hello, Fiona." His tone was dark and tired.

"Well… how are you? How was Florida?" Trying not to sound too whiney, she hated to ask the question and really didn't care how Florida was, glad that he was finally back on her home turf.

Several seconds passed before he answered. "It was fine. What do you want, Fiona?"

Pacing in her multi-million-dollar apartment in front of a panoramic view of Manhattan, she feigned innocence. "I wanted to congratulate you on the big deal you and your team landed. Daddy told me everything. I'll be at the reception tomorrow night. Do you think we can find a moment to talk? *Alone?*"

The distance between them seemed cavernous, but Fiona wasn't about to give up and turned her tone down a notch. "I've really missed you, Thomas. And I want to apologize for not being sympathetic to what you've been going through. I hope you know how sorry I am that you lost your grandfather. I should have been there for you." Chewing on her lower lip, she waited for his response. Could he see right through her?

A heavy sigh emitted from the phone. "I appreciate that, Fiona. I'll see you at the reception."

Fiona arched her eyebrow with smugness while remembering their conversation from the night before. It had been a long couple of weeks without Thomas Capshaw on her arm, and she was ready to have him back in her life again, determined to placate his sensitive-artist nature. It was up to her to lure him back into her social circle and convince him to be her boyfriend again, and ultimately, her fiancé someday. Life without him had been dull and drab. She genuinely liked Thomas and the effect his good looks and witty banter had on her circle of uppity friends. He came across as brooding and shy, which was enduring to most. But she knew she could groom him to be a successful force to be reckoned with. They could be the next power-couple of New York City together, invited to only the exclusive of parties and events, featured in the social mags and newspaper columns. His ties to his famous grandfather made him eclectic, for sure—something the elite crowd happened to love. With her, not so much. She preferred the business side of Thomas, not the long-suffering artist-Thomas. If he could just concentrate on his career in New York and put his boyish ideals to bed, there's could be a couple's goal for the ages.

Lost in a daze of longing, her cellphone pinged with a message her driver was waiting downstairs. Wrapping her bare shoulders in a mink stole, she held her satin clutch to her chest and winked at herself in the hall mirror near the front door.

"Time to get your man back." Fully confident and feeling in control, she turned on her heels and exited the posh apartment in a swing of fringe.

CHAPTER SIXTEEN

"You shaved," Emeline exclaimed staring back at Thomas from the small cellphone screen as they Facetimed. "I thought you were going full-on Leonardo da Vinci," she quipped wittily. "Did you change your mind?"

Thomas smirked and brought a hand up to his smooth jawline and shrugged. "I have to go to this work event tonight. Beards are kind of frowned upon."

"Hmmm," Emeline responded as she tilted her head and furrowed her brow. "What's going on Cappy? I thought you went straight from the airport to the office to give your notice? I guess you still have to go to work functions until you wrap things up, huh?"

Thomas hung his head in shame. How could he tell her his strategy didn't go at all according to plan? That his team was awarded the most substantial bid in firm history? If he left now, the deal might be rescinded which would cause an avalanche of heartache and embarrassment to not only his colleagues but to the entire company. Merrill-Seagram-Oliver had made the front page of the *New York*

Times that morning, not even twenty-four hours since he had left Sandersville Beach. The buzz in the world of architecture was deafening, the congratulations coming in droves.

"Emmy, do you trust me?" His question must have caught her off guard. He watched as she sat up perfectly straight and slowly nodded. Her wide eyes held a warmth he wished he could crawl through the phone and burrow into forever.

"Of course, I do. You know that."

Thomas swallowed and ran his thumb across the screen image of her beautiful face. "This might take longer than I thought. The firm…" He cleared his throat. "My team just landed a huge bid in Chicago. I need time to line everything up so my entire group won't lose out on this incredible opportunity. It's a game-changer for them and their families."

Emeline pursed her lips as if thwarting off a frown. "Oh…that's good news for them, I guess. How long will it take for you to line things up?"

Her eyes drew him in with such intensity, he couldn't help but warble. "I…I'm not sure."

The ache in his chest was real, and he fought the overwhelming urge to tell her everything—how he got the job in the first place, about Fiona, how embarrassed he was for not telling her sooner. The sudden turn of events threw him off, and he didn't know what to do. This kind of architectural success was something he would have to navigate for years, not a few months. His life with Emeline flashed before his very eyes and anger welled in his soul. He could easily walk away from his commitment to Mr.

Merrill and his demands to keep Fiona happy. But to walk away from his team was different. They were innocent. How could he let them down? This was a huge deal and unlike him, would undoubtedly push some of them up the corporate ladder where they belonged. The realization of what a poser he had been all these years slapped him hard across the face. His whole life in New York was a lie. His team was compromised of loyal, talented architects that deserved this fantastic chance. None of them, including Emeline, knew the truth about how he acquired his position in the company, and he hoped to god he could keep it that way.

"I'll know more after this week." He watched her glower on the other end and suddenly had an idea. "Em?"

"Yes, Cappy?"

"While I'm gone, I want you to stay at Cap Cottage whenever you want to. I would love knowing you were there enjoying it while I was away."

"Really?" Emeline immediately perked up.

Thomas smiled. "Yes. Absolutely! Bring some art supplies over and paint the view. Make yourself at home. You know you're going to need more paintings before your first show anyway. It would be a nice, quiet place for you to concentrate on your art."

The familiar pink spots blotted her cheeks in gladness, and he was thankful for the diversion.

"That view…" she remarked wistfully. "If you're sure it's okay."

"Absolutely." They were smiling warmly at each other

again. "Emmy, please know this isn't forever."

"I know. I just miss you so much, and it's only been a day."

"I miss you too, sweet Emeline." A reminder text flashed across his phone screen signifying it was time for him to head to the party. "I have to go, Emmy. God, I wish you were coming with me."

"Me too."

He watched her kiss the tips of her fingers and hold them up to the camera on the phone. His heart surged with love as he did the same.

***

Fiona leaned her elbow on the mahogany bar and looked around the room for the umpteenth time, her patience fuse slowly fizzling out. Where was Thomas? Sipping on a third glass of champagne, she closed her eyes and enjoyed the bubbly that ran down the back of her throat. At least her father had good taste in booze and always offered his employees the best of the best at these boring functions. The attentive wait staff passed by with yet another silver tray filled with an endless supply of hors d'oeuvres, her appetite non-existent replaced with the fluttering of butterflies and blended grapes. The Cipriani Club was a well-known establishment in the heart of the New York Financial District. The company had rented out the popular bar and terrace last minute for the impromptu celebration to commemorate the firm's latest venture. Fiona wrinkled her nose with haughtiness thinking to herself that to be fashionably late was one thing—to miss an event that was planned in your honor was quite another.

A ruckus ensued, and she could hear hearty roars of congratulations coming from the lobby where some of the staff were lined up to take coats and pass out the first of many cocktails. With an eagle eye, she watched as Thomas Capshaw entered the space, his handsome presence catching her off guard. He was dressed to the nines in a familiar designer black suit her long-time stylist had recently recommended, and his dark hair was wind-blown. Not able to put her finger on it, Fiona thought he looked different since the last time she saw him before he left for Florida. Watching him like a voyeur from across the room, she continued to sip modestly from her glass.

"Would you like another?" The bartender asked, his gaze pleased. The burly man had been attentive to her for the past hour, humoring her with little side jokes which she tittered to in response. At first, she was glad to have the distraction and attention from a handsome stranger. Now, she couldn't be bothered.

"Yes," she rudely quipped sliding her crystal glass across the bar toward him. If anything was going to get her through the night, it was definitely going to be more champagne.

The man took her glass and poured from an open bottle. "There's no reason to get snippy, Princess."

With daggers coming out of her ice-blue eyes, Fiona clenched her jaw and slowly turned to stare him down. Who the hell was he to call her, Princess? Only her father called her that!

"Now, now. Don't get your panties all in a wad," he chuckled. "I know your type. You come early to these things and get into a comfortable position before you hunt

your prey. By the looks of it, he just walked in the door."
He motioned with his head toward the group of guys
hovering around Thomas.

Fiona was astonished and had to close her open mouth
as she glared at the man. "You don't know anything about
me," she snapped before she picked up the full glass,
turned her nose up into the air and sipped.

"Whatever you say," he grinned. "Let me know if you
need anything else. And by-the-way, you should probably
eat a little something before all that bubbly goes straight to
your pretty little head."

With a swift turn, she again eyed the bartender with
venom as he walked away to tend to another couple of her
father's employees. How dare he insinuate she had too
much to drink already? It was only a couple of glasses,
wasn't it? Quickly, she set her glass down and grabbed her
clutch to pull out a compact and lipstick. Staring into the
tiny oval mirror, she eyed her reflection and turned her
head from side to side to make sure her makeup was still
on point. Everything was perfect to which she smiled
satisfactorily.

Thomas made his way slowly through the room,
stopping several times to chat with fellow team members
and their significant others. Fiona watched as a waiter
approached and handed him a bottle of beer. She also
watched him nibble on appetizers, laugh several times and
pat people on the back as they clinked cocktails in a toast.
He was caught up in a long conversation with her father,
and by the time he was close enough to make eye contact,
Fiona had consumed another two glasses of champagne
and was feeling no pain.

"Sit up straight, sweetheart. Here he comes," the

bartender whispered keenly while setting a glass of water next to her flute.

Before she could utter a rude response, she was taken aback by Thomas Capshaw's close up attention.

"Hello, Fiona." His smile was warm as he approached her with one hand in his pocket, and his full lips seemed to glisten from a recent swallow of beer.

"Hello, yourself, Thomas," she openly flirted while batting her eyelashes. "I was beginning to think you didn't want to talk to me." She patted the empty bar stool next to her. "Sit. Let's catch up."

Thomas gave a quick nod and settled next to her.

"What can I get for you, sir?" The bartender's smile glinted in the chandelier light as Fiona clenched her jaw. She did not want anyone to interrupt their conversation, especially the over-friendly bartender.

"The same, please," Thomas politely replied, holding up his beer bottle. Eyeing her empty glass, he added, "And another refill for the lady."

The bartender cocked his head as he looked at Fiona and she raised her eyebrows in response as if to dare him to deny her a refill. With a slight smile, he efficiently filled her glass to the rim, his voice rumbling with baritone thickness. "Enjoy."

"Come out to the terrace with me, Thomas, so we can have a little more privacy." Sliding off the stool, she stumbled a bit in her high heels as Thomas grabbed her by the elbow to steady her.

"You okay? How many glasses of champagne have you had already?"

Not wanting to be bothered with his inquisition, she shoved her clutch under her arm, grabbed her glass and confidently pulled him by the hand through the crowd to the double doors that led to the narrow balcony overlooking Wall Street. The brisk air hit her face, bare shoulders and arms in an instant and she inhaled sharply as if a cold bucket of water had been tossed against her skin.

"It's kind of cold out, Fiona. You sure you want to talk out here?"

Setting her things on a small table, she posed with her hands on her hips and swiveled to show off the fringe of her designer gown. "Do you like the dress?"

"Um, sure. You always look nice," he replied, shifting uncomfortably. "What is it you want to talk about exactly?"

Fiona picked up her champagne and took a sip while demurely looking over the rim at him. "You need a haircut," she blurted, eyeing his dark locks with intensity. "You know it's imperative to look your best, especially when you're the up-and-coming power couple of New York."

The words flowed effortlessly out of her mouth, and the cold air seemed charged with an intensity that perked up her mood. Approaching him, she boldly combed her long, manicured fingers through his unruly hair, and ran her tongue across her top lip, eyeing him with concentration.

"We can be that, you know. Especially now. Daddy

told me this was a huge deal. Congratulations." She thrust her glass toward his beer bottle to toast and missed, causing alcohol to spill on his shoe. "Oopsies," she giggled.

"Fiona, you're drunk. I think I need to call you a cab."

"No," she whined before throwing back the entire glass in one, large gulp. With her eyes narrowed, she stared at Thomas and boldly closed the space between them. "I only go home if you come with me…"

"Fiona…," he interrupted tersely.

"Please Thomas." She limply hung her arm over his shoulder as she used her index finger to trace his lips with the tip of her crimson nail. "Come home with me."

"Fiona, stop. We broke up, remember? This isn't going to work." He gripped her wrist as she nestled against him and stepped back.

"It can work, and it will." Her words tumbled out breathy with desire. Thomas smelled divine, and she wanted nothing more than to take him home and cuddle into the warm crevice of his neck.

"*No.*" The abrupt way he pushed back startled her. "I don't love you, Fiona. I never loved you. It's over."

Fiona could feel the cold creep into her bones as icy tears welled in her eyes. The evening had not gone as planned, and she willed herself to keep it together. Holding her woozy head high, a shiver spread through her body as she gritted her teeth in resolution. How dare he turn his back on her.

His face softened as he reached for her hand. "You're cold. Let me take you back inside…"

"*Fuck you!*" She spat dramatically, pulling away from his grasp. "Get your hands off me."

"Fiona, come on."

He reached for her again, and she turned her back to him, crossing her arms against her heaving cleavage like a sulky child.

"Okay. Have it your way. We can still be friends, Fiona. Especially with me working for your father." He paused, but she didn't dare turn around, trying desperately to maintain her dignity. "If you need a ride home, let me know. I'll be inside."

The patio door clicked shut as Fiona blinked back hot tears. With newfound tenacity, she wiped her face, grabbed her clutch and reentered the building. Thomas was already half-way across the room, and her vision warbled watching him go. She had to grip the wainscoting on the wall to make her way slowly back to the bar as a surge of rage spread new warmth through her frozen heart. How dare Thomas Capshaw refuse her?

Noticing her father seated at a corner table deeply immersed in conversation with a couple of suits, she knew now was not the time or place to give him a lecture regarding her ex-boyfriend. As she looked around at all the loud, obnoxious guests, she tried to recall where exactly the lobby was. The last thing in the world she wanted to do was embarrass herself.

"Can I offer my assistance?"

Fiona looked up into the eyes of the handsome bartender who grinned back at her. "Come on, sweetheart. Hold on to me, and I'll make sure you get to the lobby safe and sound." He offered his bulging bicep, and she accepted, thankful he was telling her what to do. Her state-of-mind was barely hanging on like a tightrope artist trying to navigate the wire in a wind storm.

"Not too fast," she slurred as she gripped his arm to steady herself, anxious to get out of there without causing a scene.

The man patted her hand with reassurance. "I've got you, Princess."

CHAPTER SEVENTEEN

Emeline handed Ginger a tall glass of lemonade and sighed with her hands on her hips, looking out at the magnificent view of the calm ocean from the Cap Cottage deck.

"Mmm, that has just the right blend of sweet and tart," Ginger said, smacking her lips after a long sip. "Aren't you going to have any?"

Emeline turned and smiled at her friend who was lounging on a sturdy beach chair, the teak wood weathered and gray. "I'll have some later. I made it for you."

"Come and sit," she nodded toward the empty chair next to her. "I want to hear all about your last conversation with Thomas and how you're doing with all this."

A slight breeze lightly caressed Emeline's face as she slunk into the chair next to Ginger, the onset of spring warming up the late afternoon. It had been two weeks since Thomas had left Sandersville Beach and she was feeling out of sorts. No matter how many hours she spent at the cottage painting or relaxing in the intimate rooms, they were still utterly empty without Cappy around.

"Any word on his departure date?"

Emeline sighed. "No, not yet."

Ginger frowned and set her glass on the small table between them. "Well, he has to have some idea, doesn't he? I mean, he's been gone for weeks!"

"Two weeks, twelve hours and...," she paused to dig her cellphone out of her pocket and look at the screen. "Forty-eight minutes."

"Oh, honey. You've got it bad." Ginger struggled to sit up and swing her swollen legs over the side of the lounge chair. "You have the stopwatch going on your phone, don't you?"

Emeline swallowed thinking to herself she was such a nerd for counting every second Cappy was away. With each passing minute, it felt like she was losing small bits of her heart, an image of confetti being tossed in the sea breeze coming to mind. "It's stupid, I know. I can't seem to paint either. Everything I put on canvas looks...stupid. Everything is *stupid*, Ginger." She could feel her eyes brim with tears. "It feels like it was all a dream..."

"What was a dream?" Ginger interrupted.

"All of it. Thomas coming back to Sandersville Beach, spending time with him, making love, laughing, hanging out together." By this time, tears were rolling down her cheeks as she gripped the edges of the chair. "After my mother died, I wasn't sure if I could stay here in this town.

When the media circus finally calmed down, it took me a long time to get back on my feet again. Everyone had their eyes on the "poor Fischer daughter," and I couldn't figure out what I was supposed to do with my life. I thought about leaving for years, but I eventually found my way. And then Thomas came back, and it was a full-circle moment. We started making plans, and I finally felt— complete." Swiping her cheeks with the back of her hand, she stared out at the water. "Ginger, what if he decides he doesn't want to come back after all? What if his life in the Big Apple has more to offer? What if I never see him again? God, I feel so *stupid*!"

"Sweetie, stop!"

Emeline blinked back the hot tears that streamed down her face and sniffled while running her hand under her nose. Ginger looked at her with a sympathetic, motherly smile and absentmindedly rubbed her pregnant belly. "I have an idea. And don't use the word, 'stupid' again. Hear me out."

"What?" Emeline moaned.

Ginger bit her lower lip to stifle a smile. "Go to New York."

"What? I can't do that," she responded incredulously. "He's busy—he won't have time for me. And besides, I've never been on an airplane. I've never even been out of the state of Florida!" The thought of traveling so far away from her hometown seemed absurd—or was it?

Ginger grinned from ear to ear with purpose. "Come on, Em! It'll be an adventure. And Thomas doesn't have to know you're coming. Surprise him! If he's as miserable as you are, which I'm willing to bet he is, the surprise will be worth it, don't you think? Sometimes it's okay to listen to your heart…"

Emeline mulled over the million thoughts in her head that swirled like tiny seashells in a riptide. To see the surprised look on Thomas's face would be memorable, for sure. Perhaps Ginger's idea wasn't so far-fetched. She stood and started for the door.

"Where are you going?"

Turning to see the shocked look on Ginger's face, Emeline couldn't help but giggle with newfound excitement. "I'm getting a glass of lemonade with a shot or two of tequila in it and a pad of paper. We're going to write down the pros and cons of your stupid idea." Her face glowed with exhilaration as she turned on her bare feet and headed inside.

Ginger bellowed from behind. "It's not stupid, you'll see!"

Twenty-four hours later, Emeline clutched a backpack on her lap with white knuckles and stared out the oval airplane window at the topography below. The view was breathtaking, the descent into La Guardia airport high above the Upper Bay of New York Harbor something she would never forget. Biting her lip, she squinted and could barely make out the tiny figure of the Statue of Liberty far below.

"Excuse me, miss?"

Emeline was startled and turned wide-eyed to the smiling flight attendant, barely able to contain her excitement. "Yes?"

"I'm sorry, but you need to put your backpack under the seat in front of you and make sure your seatbelt is fastened as we make our final approach to the airport."

Nodding, Emeline wasn't about to reveal to the attendant that her seatbelt had been tightly fastened the entire flight. The older gentleman sitting next to her slept most of the trip and now that he was awake, showed no interest in her. Shoving her backpack under the seat, she eagerly turned her back on him and resumed her gaze out the window at the incredible view.

When the flight was booked, Ginger had told her that a window seat was the "best seat in the house." Man, she wasn't kidding. It seemed surreal that she was flying high above the clouds and the ocean toward an island where millions of people thrived, one of whom was her Cappy. Breathing through her nose in a deep inhale, the romance of the window seat wasn't lost on her. Here she was risking her life flying for the first time to surprise her boyfriend in New York City. It was overwhelming, really. Ginger was the culprit, egging her on with contagious enthusiasm helping her book the flight, pack her bags and get her to the Ft. Lauderdale airport in record timing.

Her heart accelerated as the plane looked like it was about to plunge into buildings, the roar of the engine causing her eyes to widen in a panic before they touched down with a thump. Her chest was rising and falling with adrenaline, anxious to get off and find her man. Not wanting to come off as an inexperienced traveler, she confidently slung her backpack over her shoulder and pulled her duffle bag out of the overhead bin and followed the line of people in front of her. The only other time she had been in a line this long was when she had gone on a school trip to Disney World in Orlando as a kid.

The terminal was teeming with weary travelers, some of the late day flights delayed by the patchy fog. Ducking into the crowded nearby ladies' room, she patiently waited for her turn to use the facilities and wash her hands. Staring into the mirror, she couldn't help but smile at her reflection which showed off her ruddy cheeks dotted with color. She pulled a light jacket out of her backpack and shrugged it on ready to continue her adventure.

Ginger had given her explicit instructions on how to navigate the airport—just look for the signs for ground transportation. It sounded easy enough. Following the flow of people, she finally exited a sizeable revolving door to the outside world and was immediately struck by the sights and sounds of the abysmal airport scenery against the gray sky. The traffic barely moved, yellow cabs and shuttle buses inching along the asphalt among a symphony of car horns and squeaking breaks. The cold wind nipped at her face making her shrivel into her inappropriate jacket for warmth. She noticed a roped off area of people waiting in line and high-tailed it over.

"Excuse me? Is this a taxi line?"

An elderly woman wearing an enormous puffy coat and clutching a worn roller-bag turned slightly and gave her the once-over. Her New York accent was shrill. "Yeah. Don't worry, it moves fast."

"Great! Thanks."

Emeline spent the next ten minutes in line shivering while she sent a text message to Ginger back home.

Arrived safely. Waiting for a cab. It's freezing here!

Ginger replied almost immediately. *I told you to bring a*

heavier coat! Proud of you for going outside your comfort zone. Thomas is going to be thrilled!

Wish me luck!

You don't need any luck! That boy is so in love with you—enjoy! Her friend ended the text with an emoji smiley face that had hearts for eyes making her laugh out loud.

By the time she was comfortably seat-belted into the back of a warm cab, she sighed with relief knowing she would soon be in Cappy's arms. The views from the vehicle were foreign to her, and she couldn't help but crane her neck to look up at the imposing, tall buildings that obscured the sky. As they inched their way through traffic, the cabbie drove like a bat-out-of-hell when he found open pockets and cut people off causing her to cling to the oh-my-god strap in the ceiling. No wonder Thomas was so tense when he first arrived at Sandersville Beach—anyone commuting in this kind of traffic needed to decompress after such an ordeal. When they approached an enormous bridge that had cables spider-webbing in front of gothic, double arches, Emeline played tourist and snapped a photo.

"What bridge is this?" She asked loudly from behind the cabbie's shoulder.

"Brooklyn Bridge," the driver replied with a hint of an unrecognizable accent.

Emeline nodded and gawked at the famous hybrid-cable suspension bridge, her heart thumping knowing Thomas was somewhere across the water on the other side among the towers and canyons of Lower Manhattan. When the cab finally pulled up to a curb in front of the building that housed Merrill-Seagram-Oliver, she felt light-headed and giddy. Her fingers trembled as she pulled a wad of cash out of her tiny purse strapped over her shoulder and did a double take looking at the taxi meter, the fare from the airport to the firm just shy of fifty-dollars.

"Keep the change." She struggled to get out of the smelly interior with her bags in tow and paused to look up at the enormous skyscraper with her breath coming out in foggy puffs. A box truck sped by and hit a puddle of slush, sending the spray of dirty water and ice up into an impressive arc that came down right on top of her. Shocked, she stood there frozen with her arms held out from her sides, her entire body splattered with the mess. Totally embarrassed and dripping from head to toe with her mouth wide open, snickering pedestrians walked passed her. It took her a minute to move away from the curb closer to the building. She rummaged in her backpack for the first sign of fabric and wiped her face and hands off determined not to let this unfortunate blip on her adventure get her down. Swallowing hard, she shoved the wet cloth back into her pack and forged ahead, anxious to be on the other side of her surprise.

There was no one behind the security desk, and the impressive, art deco lobby was practically deserted in the late afternoon. Impressed by the old, almost romantic architecture, she still couldn't imagine Thomas working in such a stuffy nine-to-five environment. A few weeks earlier, she had snagged one of his business cards on the dresser at Cap Cottage and kept it in her wallet, thankful his New York office phone and suite number were printed on it.

The elevator climbed slowly, and her heart raced not knowing what was on the other side. When the doors opened and revealed a large reception area, the back-lit bold letters of Merrill-Seagram-Oliver welcomed her to her final destination. Tucking a loose strand of damp hair over her ear, she timidly approached the front desk and cleared her throat. A pretty, blonde woman looked up at her and immediately spoke.

"May I help you?"

The woman seemed friendly enough which was a relief. "Umm, yes," Emeline giggled, suddenly overcome with excitement. "I'm here to see Cap…Thomas Capshaw." Standing tall, she tilted her chin into the air, proud of herself for making it all the way from Florida to New York City on her own, even if she was splattered and tired.

"Thomas Capshaw? And you are?" The woman stared back at her with apprehension fixed on her expression.

Emeline leaned forward and spoke quietly. "I'm here to surprise him. He has no idea I'm coming. I'm his girlfriend." The smile she offered the woman was genuine.

The receptionist's eyes grew large, and she cocked her head in disbelief. "*You're* his girlfriend?"

Emeline swallowed. Maybe she should have found a restroom to clean up before announcing her arrival. There was no telling what she looked like after traveling all day and getting splashed. "Um…Yes. Yes, I am," she replied confidently.

"No, you're not."

Emeline was taken aback. "Pardon me?"

"You're not his girlfriend. Fiona Merrill is. Did security let you through downstairs?"

Fiona.

All the color drained from Emeline's face as she took a step backward, and her peripheral vision wavered. "I…uh… I…I should have called." She watched in disbelief as the woman picked up the phone and mashed a button.

"I'm calling security now."

The name Fiona was running through her mind as she stumbled to the elevator door, anxious to leave. But where would she go? She had just arrived.

"Ma'am? *Ma'am*! Stay right there. I need your credentials, please!" The blonde woman was standing with the phone pressed to her ear while she yelled at her. As soon as the elevator doors opened, Emeline scrambled to get on and quickly pushed the button to close the door. The last thing she remembered was the stern look on the woman's face as she shook her finger at her.

CHAPTER EIGHTEEN

Thomas drummed his fingers on the conference table as he patiently waited for the long-winded construction manager to finish up his Power-point presentation. It had been a very long week filled with endless meetings and dinners, late nights and contract signings. Ready to call it a day, he looked forward to collapsing in his empty bed and sleeping the entire weekend, away from the stress. His team was in overdrive since the news broke about their winning bid with the airport expansion in Chicago, and it was only going to get worse. It pained him to think about Emeline back at Cap Cottage by herself. They Facetimed every night when he was available, and she never ever complained about their circumstances. Vowing to make it up to her, they often talked about his grandfather's studio and how they were going to turn it into something special for the community. He meant what he said about having her paintings on display for an exclusive showing. When that showing could be scheduled, he had no clue, and his endurance waned.

"Excuse me, Mr. Capshaw?" Ms. Morse had stuck her head through a crack in the door to summon him.

"Yes?"

"I'm so sorry to interrupt. Can you please come out for a moment?"

"Sure." Thomas excused himself, thankful for the diversion and exited the conference room. "What is it?"

"Come with me. The security guard would like a word."

Puzzled, Thomas followed Ms. Morse into the reception lobby where a man in uniform stood waiting for him.

"What's the problem, officer?"

"Sorry to interrupt you, sir, but there seems to have been a security breach in the building."

"What kind of security breach?" With his hands on his hips, Thomas listened with intensity.

The guard nodded at Ms. Morse who explained. "A young woman was here about fifteen minutes ago requesting to see you. Did you have an appointment with anyone that I didn't know about?"

Thomas scratched his head. "No. I'm in with my last appointment in the conference room right now. Did she leave a name?"

Ms. Morse shook her head. "She didn't say. She looked out of place with a big backpack on, and she carried another bag. The poor thing didn't even have on a winter coat. My first thought was she might be a homeless woman who followed you in, but then she said she was here to surprise you."

"The woman claimed to be your girlfriend, Mr. Capshaw," the security guard added.

The receptionist chuckled. "I knew right then she was an imposter and immediately called security. Fiona would have a fit if anyone claimed you as their boyfriend…"

Thomas didn't hear the last few words coming out of Ms. Morse's mouth. Without a doubt, he knew it was Emeline who had just left. Sweet Emeline who had traveled all this way to surprise him. His heart fell into his stomach as he grabbed the receptionist by the forearm in a panic. "Where did she go?"

"What?"

Thomas's grip increased. "The woman! Where did she go? Is she still here?"

Ms. Morse shrugged him off and scowled. "No, she got on the elevator before I could get her credentials."

Thomas ran back to the conference room and apologized profusely as he gathered his things in a rush and mumbled something about a family emergency. In his office, he tossed everything on his desk, grabbed his coat and cellphone and hurried back to the elevators.

"Mr. Capshaw? Is everything all right? Do you know who she is?" The security guard asked.

Thomas stepped onto the elevator and turned around with a sense of urgency in his voice. "Yes! If she comes back, call me. *Please!*"

***

It was easy for Emeline to get lost in the crowd, although her backpack and duffle bag were quite cumbersome and heavy after the long travel day. Following the flow of pedestrians up Broadway, she kept the pace of the New Yorkers and turned on Liberty Street. Old man winter was still camped out in the city, and she shivered beneath her light jacket. Trying to stay upbeat about her current situation, she kept moving and thought to herself, it wasn't so bad—and she had always wanted to sightsee in a city this famous. But she was alone, and she wasn't sightseeing. And Thomas Capshaw wasn't her boyfriend. He was Fiona's boyfriend.

Fiona.

When she had first laid eyes on Fiona's name weeks before in Cap Cottage on Thomas's cellphone, she should have questioned him about it right then. But after they reunited and became inseparable while he was home, she couldn't fathom him lying to her about a girlfriend back in New York. In fact, he never mentioned dating anyone. The look on his receptionist's face said it all. Everyone knew about Fiona but her. And what was she going to do now? Her mind reeled with the news, and her heart was crushed. They had been living a lie this whole time, and Thomas knew it. How could he promise her things in the future if he kept secrets from his past? This was not the Cappy she knew and loved, and she was too embarrassed to wait around for an explanation.

The pace of the crowd slowed, and when Emeline looked up, she was taken aback by the site of a massive tower with an exterior of what looked like mirrors that reflected the sky. Walking slowly and taking it all in, she realized she was in the shadows of the Twin Towers. The 9/11 Memorial Plaza swarmed with contemplative crowds that seemed to be paying their respects. The sound of water was prevalent as she walked down a path lined with naked trees into an area interrupted by two broad areas that contained recessed pools. She had read about the memorial, and it was something she had put on her list of things to do while in the city, hoping that Thomas could shed some light on the design.

The area felt like a sanctuary of sorts—the impressive, manmade waterfalls set within the footprints of the original twin towers. The continuous stream of water flowed into the large voids that were open and visible reminders of the absence of the once tallest buildings in the world. Her heart clutched as she got closer and could make out the names of people who had perished in the attacks, honored in bronze surrounding the water. A lump formed in her throat as she ran her fingertips along the letters, pausing to pay her respects to the victims who lost their lives on that tragic day.

It was getting late, the sky turning darker by the minute with gusts of wind growing significantly colder. Definitively depressed, tired and hungry, she found a park bench away from the crowd in the green space and unloaded her bags. She sat alone, defeated by the day's turn of events. Her clothes were stained with splatters of slush, and there was no telling what her face and hair looked like. Pulling her phone out of her purse, she was astonished to see several text messages and missed phone calls from Thomas and Ginger. Not ready to face Thomas, she called Ginger who answered on the first ring.

"*Honey*! Are you okay? Where are you?"

Emeline swallowed the large knot in her throat and swiped at rogue tears. "I'm okay," she uttered, trying very hard not to break down completely. She had been through much worse, images of her smiling mother coming to mind.

"I know what happened. Thomas called me—Emmy, it's all a *huge* misunderstanding…"

"No, it's not!" She interrupted, sitting up with fresh anger. "Ginger, he has a girlfriend. He's *always* had a girlfriend. Her name is Fiona. Can you believe it? He's been lying to me this whole time. He's a fucking liar!"

"Sweetie, just tell me where you are, okay? I'm worried about you."

Emeline slouched again, gripping the phone between her frozen fingers. "Somehow I ended up at the 9/11 Memorial. It's so…beautiful." Her pent-up emotions suddenly surfaced, and she bent over her knees and cupped her forehead in her hands as she sobbed. Ginger managed to talk her off the ledge and encouraged her to find a place to warm up out of the elements. Even with twelve-hundred miles between them, Ginger soothed her frayed nerves like the sweet mamma bear she was destined to be.

"I just looked up your location, and there's a coffee shop two blocks from you. Get you a nice, warm latte and calm down. Once you warm up, call me back, and we can talk about getting you situated for the night, okay?"

Emeline nodded wearily. "Okay. You said it's two blocks down Liberty, right?"

"Yes. I'll wait to hear from you. And Emmy…"

"What?"

"Everything is going to work out, you'll see."

"Yeah, right."

The line went dead, and Emeline sat frozen on the bench for several more minutes, utterly numb by the turn of events she didn't see coming. Finally, she tiredly put her arms through her backpack straps and trudged toward the coffee shop, her muscles aching with fatigue. As she passed the reflecting pools of the memorial again, the cascading water looked like a shimmering curtain against the dramatic nighttime lighting, and the victim's names appeared to be carved in gold. Her heart was heavy and reflective, and the only thing on her mind was getting back home.

***

Thank God for Ginger McCormick! After attempting to reach Emeline by phone and a half a dozen anxious text messages, Thomas frantically turned to Ginger for help. True to form, the mother-to-be was patient and listened to his pathetic story without judging him too harshly.

"I wish you would have told her all this before you left Florida. She came a long way to surprise you, Thomas. Did you even know she's never been on an airplane either?"

Thomas gripped the phone in his hand and shook his head. The remorse he felt for not being truthful to the woman he was in love with was paralyzing.

"I know, Ginger. I'm shocked she did that for me. Please, just tell me where she is so I can find her and explain everything."

By the time their conversation was over, the sun had

set, and the cold night had fallen over the city that never sleeps. Thomas quickly made his way to the address Ginger provided which was several blocks away from the firm. Peering in through the large glass windows of the coffee shop, he could vaguely make out the back of what looked like Emeline's head hunched over a small table in the corner. Inhaling a deep breath, he entered the shop that held a strong aroma of coffee and cinnamon. He licked his lips not knowing entirely what he was going to say.

"Emmy," he started among the piercing twirl of a coffee grinder. Her head jerked to the side as she looked up at him, her eyes wide with what looked like agony. Thomas's heart fell to his feet knowing he had caused her current state of misery. "Ginger told me where you were. Can I explain?"

Without saying a word, he watched as she hurriedly bent over to pick up a duffle bag and hook her arm through a backpack that had been perched on the edge of her chair. The bag banged into his side as she rushed past him toward the door without saying a word.

"Emmy, *please!*" He followed her outside into the throngs of people heading home from work in the diverse, thriving neighborhood, the sounds of traffic rampant.

"Emeline, stop! *Emeline!*" She didn't listen and kept going, bumping into people in her haste as she ran upstream through the pedestrian flow. When he finally caught up to her, he grabbed her by the arm and pulled her into the doorway of a dry cleaner. Staring into her amber eyes, he was caught off guard by the cold, despondent look she gave him, her usually warm gaze replaced with darkness. Her face was speckled with dirt, and for the first time, he noticed the front of her clothes seemed muddied.

"I have nothing to say to you, Thomas," she raged between gritted teeth. Before he could reply, she raised her hand in the air and swiftly struck him across the cheek with a loud *thwack*. Caught off guard by the surprise blow, he was stunned and unprepared as she elbowed him in the gut causing him to bend over in immediate pain. "You're a goddamn *liar!*" Her voice bellowed, causing onlookers to smirk as they walked by.

Determined to make things right, he practically ran to catch up with her, grabbed her with two hands, and wrestled her into an old pizza joint. She seethed and panted as he stood in front of her blocking the only way out, her face flushed a determined pink.

"Leave me the fuck alone."

"*No.* Not until you hear the truth. I should have told you everything back in Florida." He took a step toward her, and she cowered, causing the smallest of three cooks behind the counter to intervene.

"Dis guy botherin' you, lady? You want me to call the cops?" His voice was reminiscent of the actor, Joe Pesci. The other two guys wiped their hands on checkered towels and bowed up in an impressive stance of tattooed muscle under their short-sleeved shirts and stained aprons.

Emeline quickly shook her head and started toward the back of the cramped eatery where she slung her bags onto a rickety chair and sat next to them. Thomas sheepishly nodded at the brood of men before he followed her.

The table was scattered with crumbs, and her chest was heaving as she looked up at him with her arms crossed defiantly in front of her. "So...talk." The unflattering, fluorescent lighting seemed to highlight remnants of tear stains on her dirty cheeks. Thomas knew he had a small window of opportunity to come clean and was grateful.

"I can't believe you came all this way to surprise me," he gently started. "Emmy, I'm so, so sorry you were given false information back at the firm…"

"False information? I know all about Fiona," she interjected resolutely.

Thomas's eyes widened. "You do?"

How could she know anything about Fiona? He had never mentioned her before.

"I saw your phone light up with her name a few weeks ago and assumed she was a coworker. A few hours ago, your receptionist told me you're a couple. How convenient for you, Thomas—a girl in every port."

Running his hand through his disheveled hair, he aggressively shook his head. "You've got it all wrong, Emmy. Let me explain."

"It doesn't matter anymore. You have a life here. You have a *girlfriend* here. God, how could I have been so stupid?" She lunged forward and spoke in a harsh whisper. "I told you everything, Thomas. *Everything!* You are one of three people in the whole world who knows what really happened the night my mother died. How could you?"

Fraught with anxiety, Thomas couldn't help the nervous tone in his voice. "I'm honored that you trusted me enough to tell me what happened, and I promised you I would take your secret to the grave. That's what best friends do. You are by far the bravest woman I ever met.

You have to know, I would never purposefully keep anything from you. Fiona is not my girlfriend anymore, okay? Yes, we dated for a time, but we broke up right after my grandfather died. Believe me when I tell you we were not together when I was in Florida—when I was with you!" Resting his forearms on the table, he inched himself closer to her, his voice low with purpose. "I never loved her, Emeline. I love you. It's always been *you*."

Her face paled at his proclamation, and he watched her lower lip tremble. More than anything, he wanted to pull her into his arms and soothe her, desperate for her to accept his truth.

"Who I am with you is who I want to be."

CHAPTER NINETEEN

"You…you *love* me?" Emeline couldn't believe the words that had just come out of Thomas's mouth.

"Yes. Yes, Emmy. I love you. I've *always* loved you."

Somehow, he managed to unhinge one of her icy hands from her chest and grip it between his warm fingers from across the table and caress the tops of her knuckles with his thumb. "We were inseparable as kids. I'm pretty sure I was in love with you back then too, I was just too young to realize it. It's my fault we lost touch. It's my own damn fault I was estranged from my grandfather. He knew we belonged together. It all makes sense now—the box of photos and leaving me Cap Cottage. He always knew Sandersville Beach was where I belonged—with you. If I had just listened to him, none of this would have happened." Very slowly and intentionally, he brought her hand up to his lips and lightly kissed her skin. "I can't be away from you for another day, Em."

Warmth slowly started to trickle back through her limbs in her light-headed state, and her cold heart began to thaw. "What does that mean exactly?"

"When you go back to Florida, I'm coming with you. This life in New York…" He waved a hand in the air and shook his head. "I can't do it anymore. This is not who I am—it's not who I want to be. I'm listening to my heart for once in my life, and that's okay."

Emeline nervously grazed her top teeth along her lower lip as she tried to understand. "Ginger said something like that too. That's why I came…"

"Dammit, Em. You deserve the truth, no matter how humiliating it is." Thomas took a deep, intentional breath before he continued. "I was bribed into my relationship with Fiona."

"What?"

"You heard me. I'm not proud of what I've done, and the consequences have been terrible. I lost sight of who I was. My grandfather tried to set me straight when he found out, but I was too pig-headed and thought I could prove him wrong. I was cocky and thought I could have my cake and eat it too. It was all a lie. I was living a *lie*…"

Gripping his hands in her own, she tilted her head and stared back at him trying to follow his confession. "What do you mean, you were bribed into a relationship with her? How?"

Thomas hung his head and proceeded to tell her the whole story—how he met Fiona in the first place and how he was lured into his prominent position and relationship with the boss's daughter with the promise of money and prestige. Now that his team had succeeded in securing the largest bid in company history, he felt trapped—his allegiance to his colleagues admirable, but a penance just the same.

"I'm mortified that I'm a fucking beck and call guy to this woman and her father. My life has not been my own for a very long time."

Emeline shook her head in bewilderment. No wonder he hadn't told her everything. He was ashamed and embarrassed. If his team hadn't gotten the Chicago deal, they could have been together for weeks by now. He made it clear that the only reason he came back to New York wasn't because of some rich girlfriend—it was because of his loyalty to his team.

"Does Fiona know about the deal you made with her father? That's pretty despicable."

"I know they're close. And I know she tells him everything. I wouldn't put it past her to be the one who came up with the whole cockamamie scheme in the first place." Thomas's face softened as he stared back at her. "I love you, Em. I'm so sorry I ruined your surprise."

Offering him a weak smile, she squeezed his hand. "I'm sorry for ever doubting you." She couldn't help but reach across the table and stroke his cheek. "Is your face okay? I slapped you pretty hard."

Thomas grabbed her fingers and kissed them. "I'm fine. I deserved that and a whole lot more." He started to chuckle. "You should have heard Ms. Morse and the security guard trying to tell me about the homeless woman looking for me…"

"Homeless woman?" she guffawed. "I got splattered with some slush. Do I really look that bad?" Embarrassed, she pushed her hair back from her face and waited for him to answer. The warmth in his contemplative gaze caused her heart to pitter-patter.

"No. You're the most beautiful woman I've ever laid eyes on, Emmy."

*

They took the subway back to his place, Thomas insisting he carry her backpack, duffle bag and a last-minute six-pack purchase on the street corner right by his apartment. By the time he got the front door unlocked, Emeline was beyond hungry and marveled at the large pizza she had carried through the city without dropping. The cooks back at the pizza place where they talked had been especially nice, congratulating them in their classic New York accents on making amends and wished them well.

"It's kind of small. Nothing like Cap Cottage back home." Thomas hurriedly set her bags down in the narrow hallway with a thud, flicked on a few lights and took the pizza box from her. She followed him a few steps into a tiny, immaculate kitchen where he busied himself grabbing plates and napkins for their impromptu dinner. "If I had known you were coming, I'd have gotten you some tequila and limes."

Emeline shook her head. "Beer is fine, Thomas." She watched as he ran the edge of a dish towel under the faucet before he approached her.

"What are you doing?" She asked, taking a step back.

His smile seemed hopeful as he tenderly held her chin in one hand and dragged the towel down her cheek with the other. "You have dried slush on your face. Hold still."

Emeline watched his resolute expression as he cleaned her face, the heat from his fingertips familiar and comforting. When he finished, he smiled causing his azure eyes to capture the light and reminding her of the sun sparkling off the ocean's surface back home.

"All better," he whispered, finally pressing his lips to hers. Her heart melted, and she wrapped her arms around his strong middle. Their first kiss in the Big Apple was everything she imagined it could be. It wasn't forced or hurried. It was slow and intentional, romantic and full of longing.

Combing her hair back from her face with his fingers spread, he licked his lips and sighed. "I can't believe you got on a plane for me. Remember when we would sit on the beach and watch the planes high in the sky, and you said you would never, ever get on one?"

She offered a slight grin. "Well, that was before."

"Before what?" He asked.

She hesitated and looked down at his solid chest, finally relieved after the long, emotional day.

"Emmy?"

When she looked back up at him, she could feel the warm flush that crossed her features, sure that her cheeks were dotted with color. "That was before I realized, I've always loved you too."

Thomas's lips quivered into a sincere smile as he pulled her tightly against his torso.

Her lips lightly touched the warm skin of his neck as

she spoke. "When you realize you love someone, you're willing to do anything to be with them. I guess that meant flying in a plane for the first time even though I vowed I never would."

"I'm glad you did. I'm so proud of you, Em."

They ate pizza by candlelight in the small living space, the flickering, romantic light casting shadows across their faces. It was odd hearing the sounds of traffic and occasional sirens from outside, the roar of the ocean non-existent. Their conversation was light-hearted, but in the back of Emeline's mind, she couldn't help but think about the loneliness Cappy said he felt all those years and what he had sacrificed for the sake of money and prestige.

"Will you miss it?" She asked, setting her beer bottle on the small coffee table in front of them.

"Miss what?" he responded, stroking her thigh.

"Will you miss the money? The city?"

Finishing off his beer in two gulps, he set his empty bottle next to hers. "No. I have some money saved up, and I can make money at the gallery in Sandersville Beach. I definitely won't miss living in a city this size. Believe me, when I tell you, I never thought it would go this far. I got caught up in trying to prove to everyone that I was worthy of my position—worthy of respect from my colleagues and my family. But the truth is, I let things get out of control. I don't deserve any respect because I've used people along the way. I used Fiona and her father to get what I thought I wanted."

"Don't forget, they used you too," she added defensively.

"I know."

"And what do you want now, Cappy?"

"You," he said, without hesitation. "Art. The ocean. God, to slow down and enjoy the little things, you know?"

"Hmmm," she replied, resting her head on the sofa and smiling back at him. "It's the little things in life that make it worthwhile."

"Yes. Being at Cap Cottage with you was magical. I had forgotten what it was like to relax and just—enjoy." Edging toward her, he cupped her cheek and gently caressed his thumb across her skin. "You brought magic back into my life. I need you, Emeline. I've always needed you. For you to come all this way to be with me... I can hardly believe you're here."

Leaning into his touch, she sighed before she stood up and offered him her hand. His masculine glow was undeniable as he looked up at her. "Shower with me?" Thomas didn't hesitate and blew the candles out in two puffs.

Standing in the tiny bathroom, they slowly and intentionally undressed each other. Emeline ogled Thomas's body and was mesmerized by the simple flex and bend of his arm muscles as he peeled away her layers. When she was in nothing but her panties and bra, he took a step back and raked his eyes up and down her body.

"I don't deserve you," he whispered, shaking his head.

Emeline reached behind her back and unclasped her bra letting it fall to the floor. "Yes, you do." She boldly grabbed his hands and brought them up to her bare bosom and indicated without words that she was all his. Thomas's eyes were wide, and his breath came out in long sighs as he fondled her breasts. She lifted the elastic of her panties and curled them down her legs so she could step out of them. Completely naked, she watched as he mimicked her and stepped out of his boxers, his engorged penis saluting her in his stance making her giggle.

He chuckled in reply. "We need to hurry up and shower because I really want to be inside you right now." He turned the knob of the shower which sprang to life.

When they were both under the spray, he lathered his hands with a bar of soap and ran his hands over her slick skin. She squirted shampoo into the palm of her hand and quickly washed her hair. Leaning her head back under the water, she couldn't help but moan as he kneeled in front of her and washed the apex of her thighs paying particular attention to her throbbing seam, the motion of his fingers sending shoots of pleasure through her lower region.

"Turn around," she heard him say. With her back turned to him, she felt his hand swiftly move her wet hair to one side, and his doused lips press against her exposed neck. His other hand stretched around her hips and snaked toward her hot seam. When his fingers flicked her firm nub, she whimpered and thrust her butt toward his hardness, spreading her legs and egging him on. When his hard dick slid slowly inside her tightness, she gasped with surprise at the fullness and immediately pulsed to his rhythm.

"This won't take long, Emmy. I'll pull out when I'm about to come."

She could only nod, her face scrunched with immense

pleasure and her hands and legs spread against the dark tile as he rode her forcefully under the deluge of water. The hard planes of his chest were solid against her back, his lips and tongue licking and suckling her skin with pleasure as she climaxed first.

"Oh, god. *Yes!*" She sputtered between breaths, her body convulsing against him with her face turned up into the water spray. His grip intensified before he abruptly pulled out and she felt a stream of thick heat cover her back. They were both panting as the water continued to rain down on them. He lathered his hands and ran them up and down her backside before he turned her around. They both continued to pant, still coming down from the intense moment, their chests rising and falling as if they had run sprints. She couldn't help but notice tiny droplets of water clinging to his dark eyelashes above his eyes the color of the sea, his penetrating gaze making her swoon.

"I love you, Emeline. I've loved you my whole life."

"Oh, Cappy."

Clinging to each other, her water slick breasts pressed into his solid chest as they stood under the lingering spray of warmth, neither one of them letting go.

CHAPTER TWENTY

There was something to be said for spending a day in New York City with the love of your life. It was as if the gods of the universe knew that Thomas and Emeline were finally together, and they purposefully dialed up the most glorious weather for them. Gone was the chill in the air replaced with the balminess of a full sun against the pretty blue, cloudless sky luring happy, buzzing New Yorkers out in droves. The dark clouds seemed to lift from Thomas too, his usual regrets and guilt replaced with joy and happiness. To finally proclaim his love for Emeline was very freeing and he couldn't help the happy hum that emitted from his lips.

They spent the day exploring his favorite hangouts in the city. Coffee at the corner shop near his apartment was foremost after lounging way too long in his comfortable bed where he explored every beautiful crevice of Emmy's body. Their conversation flowed effortlessly, like two best friends as they sipped lattes and nibbled on gigantic muffins with crumbly tops. He borrowed a pen from the barista and sketched on a napkin while she talked to Ginger back home for a few minutes. When she was finished, he handed her the impromptu sketch from across the table with a satisfied grin.

"What's this?" She asked, opening the flimsy paper along the fold. Her eyes grew large, and her smile radiated as she stared at the silly drawing he had made of the two of them sitting at a table drinking coffee with little hearts drawn above their heads. "It's perfect," she uttered, the heat from her eyes making him woozy with love.

They ambled through Central Park and enjoyed the weather with all the other city folks taking advantage of the changing season. The tree branches were still bare, but the daffodils were blooming in swaths of bright yellow along the sidewalks as happy children scampered about. Thomas held Emmy's hand, and they had to stop more than once to pet several adorable dogs on leashes. He couldn't help but reflect on the years he lived and worked in New York and had to admit that this was the first time in a long time he had ever felt this content while being in the city.

They ate a late lunch at a pub near their last tourist stop on the eastern edge of the park—The Metropolitan Museum of Art. As they stood in line to buy tickets in the gray stone building with tall columns, Thomas leaned close to Emeline's ear. "Don't get overwhelmed. This is the largest art museum in the United States and with over two million square feet of space. We can't possibly take in all the art that's inside in one day."

"I'm just excited to see my first real Rembrandt," she replied elatedly.

They wandered aimlessly hand-in-hand through the exhibits, marveling at the cornucopia of priceless works of art, artifacts, antiques, and sculptures. The Met, as it was affectionately nicknamed, was a place where Thomas often went during times of extreme loneliness where he could hide from the outside world. It was a safe place where he could discover new art and dream about his own.

They paused in the current exhibition of famous French painter, Eugene Delacroix who was dubbed one of the greatest creative figures of the nineteenth century. On display were several of his grand paintings as well as intimate drawings by the Romantic artist who was said to have a "restless imagination."

Thomas had seen the exhibition when it opened several months before and was more interested in observing Emeline's reaction as her eyes roved several large, sixteen-foot paintings with dramatic scenes depicting history as well as literature. Placing one hand on her shoulder, he pointed with his other hand and spoke quietly. "He was known for his vivid colors and brushwork. The red in this piece is magnificent."

Nodding with her mouth slightly ajar, her expression was one of wonder and appreciation. He wished he could climb into her head and know exactly what she was thinking. To share their passion in this experience of fine art with her was a dream-come-true.

Three hours later, after roaming the Egyptian and European exhibits, they finally approached the room that held the famous self-portrait of Rembrandt. It was an oil painting on canvas dating back to 1660. Thomas scanned the informational board giving Emmy a condensed version of what he was reading. "He was a dedicated self-portrait artist all his life. It says there are over forty self-portraits by him on display at different museums today."

Emmy nodded. "I can't believe I'm looking at a portrait of Rembrandt painted by Rembrandt." Her voice with tinged with breathy humor.

Wrapping his arm around her waist, he pulled her close as they admired the famous painting side by side. "I know. Isn't it incredible? I read that he painted this when he was fifty-four years old. He really wanted to depict the signs of aging on his face. Just look at his furrowed brow and the heavy pouches underneath his eyes and double chin—this is where he used a technique where he built up the paint in a higher relief to get the image he wanted."

Emeline turned to look directly at him with squinty, smiling eyes and tilted her head. "How do you know so much about this?" She asked.

Thomas chuckled and tenderly tucked her hair over her ear. "I've spent a lot of hours in this place by myself. It's fun to see something and then do research on what you saw. It's even better when you come back after doing the research and looking at it again with fresh eyes."

"Hmmm," she responded as if she understood. "And I'd like to add that it's even more fun to look at it with someone you love."

Thomas could feel warmth creep up the back of his neck and happily squeezed her closer. Sliding his arm up and over her shoulder, he pointed at the painting again as other art connoisseurs stood nearby. "I learned that they recently removed a synthetic varnish that was on this piece."

"Really?" she replied, staring straight ahead at the self-portrait.

"Yep. When the varnish was removed, it revealed more of Rembrandt's painting method. Look at the curls of his hair spilling out from under his cap. He would take his paintbrush and flip it in a way that scored the butt end of the brush into the canvas making it look rough. Does that make sense?"

Emeline turned to him again with her mouth agape. "Are you making this up?"

"No, I swear!" He grinned back at her. "I once had a tour guide explain Rembrandt's method. It was fascinating."

"Yeah. Kind of makes me want to get back to my tiny studio and play around with some paint," she admitted.

They stood for another minute before Thomas spoke in a low tone. "Speaking of playing around. Are you ready to get out of here?"

"Uh-huh." She turned and placed a chaste kiss lightly on his lips.

Thomas licked the aftermath of her kiss and sighed. "What was that for?"

Staring up at him with her whiskey eyes glowing, she hesitated. "I...I wanted to thank you for bringing me here to this place. It's incredible." Her gaze deepened. "I wish I could have come with you before, so you weren't all alone."

Thomas understood what she was saying and agreed. "I wish that too. But you're here now. And I'm not alone anymore, Emmy, thanks to you."

Laying her head in the crevice of his neck, she nuzzled him as the museum crowd buzzed around them and whispered, "Take me home. Take me back to Cap Cottage."

***

Fiona sat dejectedly in the over-sized spa chair waiting patiently for her nails to dry in the upscale salon while listening to her chatty friend give a lackadaisical and somewhat boring version of a pep talk.

"Seriously, Fiona. Don't give up. I've known you for a very long time and you, of all people, are never one to give up!"

Holding her left hand out, Petra seemed to admire her freshly painted nails and inadvertently showed off the massive rock on her finger. The facets of the expensive diamond caught the light and caused Fiona to scowl with jealousy. Sure, it was easy for her friend to say those things. She didn't have to worry anymore because she was recently engaged to a successful business tycoon and already in the throes of planning a colossal summer wedding. Fiona should have been the one with a ring on her finger by now, not Petra. If only Thomas had followed through and had secured his grandmother's ring before his grandfather died, things could have been drastically different.

"Are you still going to come to our engagement party? I could always set you up with my cousin if you need a date."

Fiona rolled her eyes to keep her anger in check. "No thank you," she managed to mutter. A smiling hostess walked by offering champagne to which Fiona waved her off without a word.

"What? None for you today? Good god, Fiona, you really are miserable," Petra laughed, eagerly taking a flute of pink bubbles off the tray. "Thank you," she offered with a snobbish tone.

"For the record, I'm never drinking champagne again," Fiona mumbled, sinking lower into the comfortable chair.

Petra licked her plump lips and giggled. "Well, when you go overboard like that at your father's company party, I don't blame you."

Fiona recalled the horrific celebration when she drank herself into a tizzy. That was the night she was tragically rejected by Thomas. Not only was her heart crushed, the champagne hangover she experienced the next day was so intense, she thought she might die. But then Thomas miraculously called her later in the afternoon to make sure she was okay. That one act of chivalry made her more than determined not to throw in the towel. If he called to check on her, perhaps she could coerce him into accompanying her to Petra's engagement party? It was worth a shot.

"Where are you off to? I thought we were going shopping?" Petra asked, setting her flute on the small table next to her spa chair and sitting up.

"I almost forgot. My father's birthday is coming up. I think I'll stop by his office and probe him for gift ideas." Fiona put her arms through her coat that the tech held open for her, careful not to bump her fresh manicure.

"Yeah, right. You're going to the office to spy on Thomas."

"Am not."

"You are too!" Petra laughed.

Fiona cautiously picked up her designer purse with the tips of her fingers and sighed. "Well, maybe I am. He was so thoughtful calling me the day after the office party to see how I was feeling. I've kept my distance and allowed him some space. I suppose it's time I apologize to him in person."

"Hmmm, in person?"

Fiona cocked her brow and couldn't help the sly smile that crossed her lips. "Yes, in person." Turning on her expensive, heeled boots, she waved over her shoulder. "I'll call you later, Petra."

CHAPTER TWENTY-ONE

The weekend spent with Emeline felt like a dream. It was hard to leave her in the early morning, the mere sight of her sprawled asleep and half-naked across his bed tempting him to play hooky. Locking the door behind him, Thomas didn't seem to mind his commute to work that Monday morning, shoulder to shoulder with all the other suits and briefcases in the subway tunnels under Manhattan.

A perpetual smile was plastered on his lips, his mind a long roll of film replaying snapshots of the weekend spent with his best friend. Everything made sense now—his past, his present, and his future. He had scheduled a meeting with Mr. Merrill right after lunch through his assistant and waited patiently for the long morning filled with nonstop work to end. It was time for him to cut ties with the Merrill family and the firm—time for him to have his life back on his own terms. After talking it over with Emeline all weekend, he was convinced his team would be just fine without him—they were a talented bunch of professionals and also an integral part of winning the Chicago bid. The firm would be insane if they let this opportunity slip through their fingers.

His office phone lit up, and he answered on the first ring. "Thomas Capshaw." He listened as Mr. Merrill's assistant told him he was ready for their meeting. "I'll be right there." He hung up the phone and stood, his stomach suddenly full of butterflies. Buttoning his suit jacket, he inhaled deeply and confidently strode down the hallway to his boss's office and knocked twice.

"Come in, come in, Thomas!"

Shutting the door behind him, Thomas approached the enormous desk and waited patiently with his hands behind his back. Mr. Merrill finished scribbling something on a document before plucking his reading glasses off his face and grinning up at him. "Please, have a seat."

Thomas nodded and sat in the stiff wingback chair across from him, nervously clasping his hands in his lap.

"What seems to be the trouble? My assistant made it sound like this was an emergency?"

Shifting in the chair, Thomas decided to get straight to the point. "I've made a decision, Mr. Merrill. I'm leaving Merrill-Seagram-Oliver and moving back to Florida."

The old man's eyebrows raised reminding Thomas of a similar look his daughter, Fiona often held. In the past, this foreboding expression would have intimated him. But after everything he had been through, Thomas was filled with determination and unconcerned by the man's exaggerated frown.

"It's not working for me. I was going to come to you before we landed the Chicago contract, after Fiona and I broke up…"

"So, this is because of my daughter?" He brusquely interrupted.

"Yes—and no. Sir, with all due respect, I appreciate what you've done for me over the years—the rapid climb up the corporate ladder, the awesome team I've had the pleasure of leading, even the corner office. But you and I both know I don't deserve any of it. Let's face it, I didn't get here because of my exemplary architectural skills." He watched Mr. Merrill huff and cross his arms against his chest.

"You made it very clear that I would be rewarded if I continued to keep your daughter happy. I shouldn't have done that. Don't get me wrong, I've enjoyed spending time with Fiona, and I've learned so much from you and the upper management of the firm during my time here. I thought maybe I'd learn to enjoy my position in leadership in a company this big. I even mulled over the idea that Fiona might be the one for me. But the truth of the matter is, I don't love her, sir. I never have. I've finally realized why I've been so miserable all these years. I'm in love with someone else—my best friend growing up. And I want to be with her in Florida, where I belong."

The old man stood abruptly and turned his back on Thomas to look out the expansive window overlooking Wall Street. It took him a long time before he spoke.

"I had such high hopes for you, Thomas. You proved yourself worthy of your title by landing that Chicago bid with your team. You're a leader whether you want to admit it or not, and extremely talented, I might add. Fiona has told me over the years that she thought you seemed unhappy at times and she could never understand why, chalking it up to your sensitive artist mentality. You had a great job, a beautiful girlfriend and a circle of high-class friends, and yet you still weren't happy. I just don't understand. Most men would sacrifice everything to be in your position. You had it all, Thomas." Mr. Merrill turned and looked at him with narrowed, beady eyes like a cat on the prowl. "We had a deal. If I need to sweeten the pot, so be it…"

"Sir, I don't think you heard me. I don't love Fiona, I'm in love with someone else. You can't buy my love for your daughter. I finally realized I belong in Florida. It's my home, and it's where the love-of-my-life has been all this time."

"Two million dollars."

"Wh…*what?*"

"You heard me. I'll give you two million dollars to marry my daughter and stay at the firm. Think of it as a bonus for winning the Chicago contract. Do we have a deal?" The old man dared to stick his hand out for a handshake.

Thomas ran his hands through his hair with his mouth agape. "Why are you bribing me with two million dollars? This is your daughter we're talking about, Mr. Merrill. I don't want your money. I want my life back, on my own terms. Don't you want Fiona to be happy and in love with someone who loves her back? Why in the hell would you be willing to pay me that amount of money to stay with her?"

Mr. Merrill came from around the desk and got into Thomas's face. "*Because she's all I have,*" he whispered passionately. "When her mother died, I wanted to die too.

But I had a precious baby girl that my late wife adored, and I made a solemn vow that I would keep her happy, no matter what it cost me. She's happy with you, Thomas. All she talks about is you—Thomas this and Thomas that. Fiona loves you, and it will kill her to lose you. If I can do something about it, you're damn right I'm going to!"

"But she's already lost me!" Thomas yelled back. "She's a lot stronger than you think, sir. And what if she found out, huh? How would that make her feel knowing her father bribed her ex-boyfriend to stay with her? To marry her?" Thomas shook his head aggressively. "I'm ashamed I rode her coattails all these years, and I sincerely apologize for doing that. But I am not about to accept two million dollars to stay with a woman I will *never* love!"

The conversation was heated, and neither of them heard the door open until an audible gasp made them turn their heads toward the sound.

"Fiona," Thomas managed to say, his speech warbled with shock.

Mr. Merrill strode quickly to his daughter and reached for her, but she stepped back with disgust. "I never would have believed it if I hadn't heard it for myself," she gasped, incredulously.

"Fiona, Princess, let me explain…"

"Explain what, Father?" She interrupted, her painted lips quivering in anger. "All this time, you've been coercing Thomas to be with me? You…you gave him a career he didn't deserve in exchange for being my boyfriend?"

Thomas took a step forward in Mr. Merrill's defense. "Fiona, I tried…"

"Shut up, Thomas! *I hate you*," she spat. "I hate what you've done. I hate what you made me believe all these years." Her face turned red and noticeable tears started to stream down her cheeks ruining her usually perfect, made-up face.

Thomas took a step back and hung his head in shame. He deserved the tongue-lashing. In hindsight, none of this was fair to Fiona. But she wasn't completely innocent either. The woman played hardball too and never let up on him, suffocating him with her plans and demands. This whole game should have been shut down from the get-go—that he let it go this long was unforgivable.

"Fiona, darling. Please, calm down. Come and sit." Mr. Merrill tried his best to coax her into a seat, but she wasn't having it.

"No! You're as much to blame as Thomas, Father. I can't…I can't believe you both lied to me."

By this time, Fiona was sobbing uncontrollably and held her wrist to her mouth in obvious anguish. Thomas knew she could be a total diva, often exploding in emotional outbursts to get what she wanted. But this was different. This was real and something he had partially caused, and it pained him to see her suffering.

Mr. Merrill paced and gripped the back of his neck as if unsure what to do. Thomas decided to take matters into his own hands. "Sir, do you mind leaving the room for a minute, so I can have a word with Fiona alone?"

Mr. Merrill looked at his daughter for approval. "Are you okay for me to leave, Princess?"

"I don't care what you do," she sniffled, collapsing in one of the wingback chairs positioned in front of his desk. Mr. Merrill tentatively leaned down and lightly kissed the top of her head, obviously distraught.

"I'll be right outside if you need me." His voice was low and deflated, and his shoulders slumped as he exited the office.

Thomas knelt next to Fiona and offered her a tissue. They remained silent for a minute before he started to talk. "Do you remember when we went to your family's mountain house in Vail last winter?" He started.

Fiona huffed and wiped her eyes that had noticeable mascara residue smeared around them. "What about it?" Her voice was hoarse from crying.

"I wanted to check out some of the art galleries in town, remember? There were actually several things I wanted to do with you, but like always, you had an agenda of your own and shrugged off my requests every time I brought them up."

"What does this have to do with my father and you lying to me, Thomas? This is ridiculous!" She squirmed uncomfortably in her seat as Thomas stood.

"We never did anything I wanted to do. All these years, it was always about you. It's always been about you, Fiona."

Sitting in the chair next to her, he leaned his elbows on the tops of his thighs and clasped his hands together. "I knew I could never compete with you, so I didn't try. You're such a strong, confident personality. I don't know if you ever noticed, but I've been a pretty miserable, lonely person. We never talked about it. You were too busy with your plans, Fiona. *Your* plans. I went along with them because I didn't know what else to do. I was a fucking coward."

Sitting up straight, he held the arms of the chair. "I was placating your father and you. I was a beck-and-call guy, a god-damn cabana boy. Don't blame him for this. This is all my fault. I shouldn't have dated you and accepted promotions at the company at the same time. I should have earned my place in the firm like everyone else. I should have had the balls to stand up for the things I wanted out of our relationship."

"Apparently, there never was a relationship, Thomas. It's all been a lie...," she bemoaned.

"That's not true. We had some fun, and I tried, Fiona. I really tried to make you happy. The only problem was, *I* wasn't happy—and it wasn't because of you or my career. I was depressed, and I felt trapped. I missed home. I missed my grandfather and the beach. You never cared about my family or my passions. Don't you see? It never would have worked out between us. We're total opposites."

Fiona seemed to mull over his comment and pouted. "But opposites attract..."

"Come on, Fiona. You were always trying to change me, telling me how I should look and present myself. You practically picked out my entire wardrobe and insisted on redecorating my apartment against my will."

"But you said you liked my style and never complained."

"I know. And I'm sorry." They both sat in silence for

several seconds before Thomas attempted to bring some levity into the harsh conversation with a little joke. "I should have spoken up, especially after the time you made me wear that captain's hat to your friend's yacht party."

Fiona shook her head and tried to hide a slight smirk at the recollection. It was as if he was finally getting somewhere and had cracked her surface.

Looking intentionally into her tear-stained face, he spoke very slowly and changed the subject. "Your father loves you, Fiona, without a doubt. He would give you the moon if he could. You know my own father died when I was young, and I adored my grandfather. In a way, your father was like a surrogate to me while I lived here. I wanted to please him—he wanted to please you. It got way out of control, and I'm so fucking sorry."

Gently, he picked up her hand from the arm of the chair, and she didn't resist. "Fiona, we had some fun times. But I'm not the guy for you. You deserve a man like your father who will go to great lengths to move heaven and earth for you."

Fiona was staring at their hands entwined together, silent tears rolling down her face again. She sniffled and slowly pulled away from him. "Who is she?"

"Who?" Thomas replied, unsure of what she was asking.

"Who is the girl in Florida you're in love with? Have you been with her all this time?" She insinuated.

"No. No. I ran into her when I went back to Florida to take care of my grandfather's estate. We were best friends growing up and lost touch when I went off to college."

"So, you weren't cheating on me?"

Thomas bit his lower lip in amazement. After all the things that had been said, the only thing she was worried about was him cheating on her? After her father not five minutes ago offered him two million dollars to marry her? The utter hypocrisy of it all must run in the family.

"No, Fiona. We were already broken up when I went to Florida, remember? Emeline and I were out of touch while you and I were together."

"Emeline?" Her voice was suddenly laced with a shade of mockery. "That's a very country-bumpkin kind of name. I can just picture her in overalls throwing slop to the pigs on her farm…"

"*Fiona,*" Thomas's tone warned in a low rumble.

Feigning innocence, she rolled her eyes and tilted her chin up, the next question out of her mouth catching him off guard. "And how do you know Emeline's the one for you?" The piercing blue of her eyes glistened with wetness, her question stripped away of any snobbishness. They were finally talking—really talking, and he was relieved to tell her the truth. He could only hope she might believe him.

"I've always loved her, Fiona, but I didn't realize it till I saw her again. She was the missing piece in my life. To finally be together is a miracle. I need to be with her. I need to go home."

She ran her finger under her nose and nodded. "Then go. You deserve to be with someone you love. Go, Thomas."

"You deserve love too, Fiona." He waited for a beat before he stood and held his hand out to help her up. It surprised him that she took it.

Up close, her frowned expression only enhanced the lines around her mouth, her usual perfect makeup streaked like a watercolor painting. "You were my first love, Thomas."

Thomas shook his head in bewilderment, astonished that after all this time, Fiona picked this moment to profess her love for him.

"Believe me, you'll get over it," he reassured. He watched her swallow and was taken aback when she thrust herself into his chest and clung to him in a final, desperate hug.

CHAPTER TWENTY-TWO

It took Thomas over a week to organize and hand off his work-load to his team. The hardest part was putting Emeline on a plane home with a promise to join her as soon as he could. Mr. Merrill promoted one of his colleagues to his position, and the transition went off without much of a fuss. The old man didn't have much to say to him during his final exit, his frown an indication that he was none too pleased with the outcome.

Thomas never mentioned the two-million dollar offer to Emeline. It was never important to him and he didn't want to upset her with any more Fiona drama. When it was all said and done, he walked away, confident he had made the right decision to leave his life in New York. He was finally going home.

When he walked off the airplane into the Ft. Lauderdale terminal, he scanned the crowd just past the secured area and could see Emmy's head bobbing up and down as she looked frantically through the mob. Raising his hand, he captured her attention with a wave. As he got closer, the poignant look on her face conveyed pure happiness, and his heart gushed with love. Dropping his bags to the floor, he held out his arms, and she leaped into his embrace, wrapping her legs securely around his middle while making an audible squeal. Swinging her around, their lips found each other, and they frantically kissed as if they had been apart for months.

When she pulled back from him, her eyes were squinted in a broad smile, the amber warmth of her gaze a heady welcome he would never forget.

"Hi," she whispered, before biting her lower lip. Her fingers clutched the back of his neck as his hands slid down to cup her buttocks covered in denim.

"Hi." He tilted his head and couldn't help the broad smile illuminating his face. People passing by grinned and nodded as they witnessed the couple reunite. "I missed you."

She nodded vigorously and wrapped her arms around his neck, cradling his head with her hands.

"I missed you more," she said in a low voice. The puff of affectionate air that emanated from her lips caressed his earlobe causing his manhood to stir. Setting her down, they linked arms and walked to the baggage claim area. Emeline clung to him, and he couldn't help but feel immense pride walking through the airport with her by his side.

During his last week in New York, he made a deal with his landlord to get out of his lease, making him an offer he couldn't refuse. Thomas didn't want any of the furniture— not one piece. The high-end sofa, tables, rugs, and lamps were of no use to him anymore. Besides, they were all picked out by Fiona, and he wasn't remotely interested in bringing anything that reminded him of her back to Sandersville Beach. He shipped a few sentimental items and clothing back to Cap Cottage. The rest, he managed to stuff into a few suitcases and a computer bag, his uncomplicated move from New York City to Florida complete.

He and Emeline chatted non-stop during the drive back in the worn sedan she had borrowed from Rusty and Ginger. He had mentioned buying a small car as soon as he got home, but Emmy shrugged off that idea, reminding him that Sandersville Beach was a bike town. With the weather getting warmer, they could get around the one-stoplight town on bikes and really didn't need a car right now.

The familiar landscape and Southern sky were a welcome change from New York City. Spring was in the air, and he laughed as Emmy opened the sunroof and stretched her arms into the air, looking like she was at the top of a roller coaster ready to ride the first downhill curve, her animated features enhanced by the afternoon sunlight. His breath caught in his chest when he realized he was finally living his life on his own terms, the future as bright and beautiful as the sunshine coast.

When they finally pulled up into the drive at Cap Cottage, Emeline seemed keyed up and told him to leave his stuff in the car for the time being. Apparently, she had a surprise waiting for him and reached her hand out to him, pulling him forward with a sense of child-like excitement. Walking through the doors, he gawked as he looked around.

The living area was warm and inviting with a new throw casually draped over the side of the sofa adorned with pillows in vibrant colors. Two artist easels were positioned back to back in front of the large, unobscured window, the blinds completely opened to show off the magnificent view of the ocean. A small table was pulled up close to one of them, and Thomas could see remnants of paint on a color wheel, the first strokes of a piece coming into form on white canvas. The wicker bookshelf was full of textured treasures including cobalt blue glass bottles and balls, shells and sea stars—the nautical theme perfect against the wrap around water view from the windows.

He paused to turn and look at her finished piece on the wall he had bought. *Run to the Sea* held the same beauty and mystery as the first time he laid eyes on it. Knowing its history, he felt great satisfaction that it was finally in a safe place where it belonged among the other unexpected treasures, the past finally put to bed.

Emeline was watching him intently, the look on her face, beseeching. "Come in here," she said tugging his hand in the direction of the bedrooms.

As she pulled him past the kitchen, he couldn't help but notice the potted, purple violets situated on the thin ledge of the windowsill and an assortment of ripe fruit sitting in a large bowl on the counter. Cap Cottage was full of life and love. When they got to the doorway of his grandfather's master suite, Thomas did a double-take. Gone was the hospital bed and in its place, a queen-size mattress set flush against an ornate, iron headboard. A small lamp was glowing on the bedside table as the ceiling fan turned lazily above the quilted bedspread and oversized pillows. The whole room was inviting and romantic causing Thomas to shake his head in wonder.

"What have you done, Emmy?"

Her entire face fell. "You don't like it? I can always take

it back—"

"No," he interrupted. "I love it. How did you manage to do all this?"

He watched as her cheeks dotted with color and she looked at the floor. "I wanted to surprise you. I wanted you to feel like you were finally home when you got back from New York."

Thomas held his hand against her cheek and pushed his fingers into her hair, tenderly holding her face. He loved this woman with every fiber of his being, her gift more precious to him than she would ever know. "When I'm with you, I'm home." He pulled her forward and kissed her on the forehead. "Thank you for this. I love you."

"You're welcome," she smiled. "And I love you too." Before he could say another word, she squealed, ran to the edge of the bed, and jumped on top of the mattress. "Come on Cappy. We need to christen our new bed properly."

Thomas grinned from ear to ear and quickly unbuttoned his shirt. Shrugging it off, he dramatically threw it to the side. With two long strides, he sprang onto the bed and straddled Emeline as she giggled uncontrollably on the soft fabric. Staring into her heated gaze, the contentment he felt was overwhelming. Thanks to his grandfather, he was finally in a home he loved and reunited with his best friend who turned out to be the love of his life. It was time to leave the past in the past and start living his dream.

***

"Well, this is quaint. I never thought of a hatchback as

a luxury automobile." Fiona's friend, Petra adjusted the expensive sunglasses over her eyes and watched the rental car guy load their designer suitcases into the back.

"It's fine, Petra. This is all they had left on such short notice. It will get us from point A to point B. Think of it as an adventure, okay? We talked about this on the plane. I looked up Sandersville Beach online and found us a hotel. It's kind of remote so don't expect anything high end." Fiona dug into her handbag and pulled out a five-dollar bill to tip the man.

Petra put her hand on her hip as if waiting for him to open the passenger side door. When he didn't, she huffed and opened it herself. When she was situated, she looked around the car with disgust. "Tell me why you're doing this again?" Her voice was laced with irritation.

Fiona turned the key in the ignition, fastened her seatbelt and adjusted the rearview mirror. It had been a while since she had driven a car. "I told you, I just need to see this woman—"

"Emeline?" Petra interrupted. "What kind of name is that anyway?"

Coming from a woman named after a tourist city in Jordan, Fiona couldn't help but snicker. "I have no idea." Looking from left to right, she slowly eased out of the parking space and sighed. "I need to know what she's like. Is she pretty? Does she work? What does she have that I don't? I couldn't find her on any of the social networks. Thomas said they grew up together. They were best friends or something like that. Wouldn't you have thought he would have mentioned that while we were dating?"

"Hmm, I suppose. Will you try to talk to her?"

"No. Definitely not. I would like to speak to Thomas though—to make sure he's certain he made the right decision."

"Oh, look! Palm trees!" Petra pointed toward a row of the tropical trees, seemingly disinterested in the conversation. "Didn't you say our hotel was right on the beach? I hope we get there in time to lay out by the pool. This weather is gorgeous."

Fiona didn't say anything and kept her focus on driving. The tension in her shoulders radiated up into her head and had caused an annoying headache for the past week. When she finally made her mind up to fly to Florida, Petra was her first call. Her friend was more than happy to accompany her flying first-class, especially after the unexpected spring blizzard that recently covered New York. The promise of sunshine and cocktails with little umbrellas in them sealed the deal. It was a miracle they made it out of La Guardia Airport. Thank god for plane de-icing.

After a while, the sunny weather seemed to soothe her haggard nerves. She intended to have closure with Thomas Capshaw but not before she laid eyes on his love interest. If she could just see this woman and assess her competition, maybe she could understand and move on with her life. On the other hand, seeing Thomas with someone else on his arm could send her into a tizzy, and she hoped she could keep her rage in check.

Two hours later, they checked in to a quaint boutique hotel on the far south end of Sandersville Beach. The fresh sea breeze whipped at their hair as they fumbled with their oversized luggage into the lobby. The interior of the place was sparsely furnished, the modern angle with high end fixtures a relief. As Fiona checked them into the fifth floor "penthouse" suite, Petra disappeared into a lounge and came back out a few minutes later with two sparkling glasses of champagne. Fiona's self-imposed alcohol time-out was officially over.

"Oh, yes!" she remarked excitedly, taking one of the flutes.

"They didn't have Cristal, so it will have to be Dom Perignon for the weekend," Petra lamented, holding her pinky finger out and smelling the top of the alcohol.

"Cheers." Fiona didn't care what brand of champagne they drank as long as it was cold and had alcohol in it. She clinked her glass with Petra's and slowly sipped, savoring the explosion of tiny bubbles on her tongue. Being at their final destination after the long travel day, she had to admit, she was thankful for her friend's appreciation for a decent happy hour.

Their room was not at all what Fiona expected. She assumed it would be rustic being off the beaten path and was pleasantly surprised when they entered the expansive, tastefully decorated sitting area that opened up to a large balcony overlooking the beach. Breathing in the pungent scent of the salty ocean, she closed her eyes and allowed the wind to blow her hair back as the sun penetrated her face. Her body tingled, knowing she was close to Thomas. The very thought of seeing him again made her heart palpitate, but she needed a few more glasses of bubbly and a good night of beauty sleep before she attempted to track him down.

"This weather is glorious. Put on your suit and let's go lay by the pool with another cocktail."

Petra held a solid white bikini in her hands, and her huge diamond glinted in the sunlight, causing an immediate ache in Fiona's heart. The engagement ring was a stark reminder of what she missed out on with Thomas. The sudden urge to lie in bed and pull the covers over her head was tempting. Instead, she tilted her chin up with resolution and looked on the bright side. It had been a long time since she had been on a beach getaway. The change of scenery was already soothing her broken spirit. In due time, she would have closure and find out what this Emeline girl was all about. As soon as she relaxed and took full advantage of her father's platinum credit card, she'd find out one way or another.

"You go on. I want to unpack and finish this glass. Meet you down there?" She offered Petra her most sincere smile with her perfect eyebrow arched diffidently.

Her friend smirked before she turned on her heels toward the bedroom, her tight ass swinging with purpose. "I'll get the bartender to chill us a bottle. God, I'm so glad to be out of the city!"

Fiona was thankful to have a few minutes on the balcony to ponder her decision to come to Florida. Sipping from her glass, she looked out across the ocean. The waves formed small white caps further out, and the colors changed from a deep blue to a greenish sapphire rimmed in a white froth as the water surged onto the shoreline. Only a few people walked along the beach, and it was hard to imagine this was the place Thomas grew up. Why didn't she care before? Why did she bother now? Did she truly love him or was it a competition to win him back?

Draining the glass in one gulp, she grimaced, thinking about her father. If he hadn't meddled in her relationship with Thomas, none of this would have happened, she was sure of it. Knowing how sensitive Thomas was, she should have been more in tune with some of his needs and promised herself she would try harder moving forward. Perhaps if he saw a change in her, he might reconsider and come back to New York. But then there was the matter of love. He said he didn't love her—he loved Emeline.

With a heavy sigh, Fiona conceded and went inside, her head starting to pound again. She needed to distance herself from her own feelings and relax for the rest of the day. A bottle of Dom with her friend just might do the trick.

CHAPTER TWENTY-THREE

Emeline paused at each photo hanging from the twinkle lights in Lawrence Capshaw's gallery, the images of her and Thomas through the years conjuring up vivid memories. The beautiful, romantic scene he created for her weeks ago was coming down that day to make room for her paintings, the reality of her very first art exhibit looming near. She knew she was dawdling, but she couldn't help it. Thomas had picked close to one hundred photos to hang in the space, and she wanted to look at all of them again before they were put away. The box with the red lid had been brought back and sat against the wall, ready to be filled with the hanging photos for safe keeping.

Pulling one of her favorites from the clothespin, she studied the black-and-white picture closely and had to stifle a smile. They were in their bathing suits standing on the beach. Thomas had his arm draped casually over her shoulders, as best friends often do, and she was leaning her wet head on his cheek, holding his fingers with her hand. They must have been in their early teens, their hair and skin golden from the sun and their smiles beaming with innocent love.

Thomas was right. They had always loved each other, the subtle proof displayed in their expressions in each and every photo fluttering in the room. Sliding the picture into the front pocket of her worn overalls, she couldn't help herself and plucked another one off the line. An idea had formed, and she decided she wanted to put a couple of their vintage photos on the refrigerator back at the cottage, and maybe on their bathroom mirror. Perhaps she should scan them all and create an online scrapbook? They could look back on these abundant moments in time his grandfather captured on film and cherish the memories and the stories that went with them, together—forever.

Thomas was at the coffeehouse ordering caffeine for the long work day ahead. With him finally back in town for good, he seemed anxious to clean out the space and prepare for the grand re-opening with a special night honoring his grandfather's work followed by a few weeks highlighting her art. It was a-dream-come-true for a girl like Emeline. The community she lived in that witnessed her mother's horrific demise didn't have to feel sorry for her anymore. It was a chance at a fresh start—for people to see her talent up close and in an exhibition. It was all very surreal to her. Everything that happened as of late in her life felt like a dream, and she often pinched herself to make sure she was wide awake for it.

As she pulled down several more photos, she heard the front door of the gallery open on squeaky hinges and turned around, half expecting to see Thomas with to-go cups in hand. Instead, an attractive woman tentatively entered and nosily looked around. She was way overdressed for the beach, wearing what seemed like an expensive pantsuit and high heels. Her designer handbag was nestled in the crook of her elbow, and her makeup was flawless—her red lips a stark contrast against her blonde hair and ice-blue eyes.

"May I help you?" Emeline asked curiously.

"Umm, yes. Is this the Lawrence Capshaw Gallery?"

Emeline could hear a hint of a northern accent in the woman's speech and nodded as she approached her. "Yes, it is. But I'm afraid we're not open at the moment."

"Oh, I'm not here to look at any pictures," she said, eyeing the photographs attached to the twinkle light wires with disinterest. "I'm here to see Thomas Capshaw, Lawrence's grandson?"

Something in Emeline's gut triggered, and she suddenly knew who this woman was. Her face paled as she paused a few seconds more, taking in the image of Thomas's former New York girlfriend, intrigued that she was so well-put-together and professional-looking. Fiona's eyebrow rose impatiently, and her red lips were clenched in a tight smile.

"You're Fiona, aren't you?" Emeline blurted knowingly. The woman's brow creased in confusion and her narrowed eyes held disdain as she took a step back.

"I'm Emeline." Saying her name out loud to this woman sounded like a confession of sorts—as if she were guilty of something even though she knew she wasn't.

Fiona scowled as if repulsed before she recovered with a fake smile. "Yes, I'm Fiona Merrill. Can you please tell me where Thomas is? I'd like a word with him if you don't mind."

Emeline tucked the photos she had been holding in her hands into her overalls and nodded. "He's just down the street getting coffee. I can run and get him for you."

"I would appreciate that very much," she replied, matter-of-factly.

The two women were in a standoff, each eyeing the other with interest. The contrast between them was laughable. Emeline was dressed in work clothes stained with paint splatters, ready to do manual labor all day. Her hair was piled high on top of her head in a frizzy messy bun and there wasn't a stitch of makeup on her tanned face. The apex of her thighs still tingled from the fantastic sex she and Thomas had an hour earlier—a reminder that he was in love with her and not Fiona Merrill. Her inner goddess couldn't help but do a fist pump.

Fiona, on the other hand, looked like she had just stepped out of a high-end salon. Her makeup was heavy, and Emeline thought she might be wearing false eyelashes. Her chic bobbed hair was flat ironed and probably loaded with anti-frizz products to fend off the Florida humidity. Even though her taste was impeccable, she couldn't help but think this woman looked lonely and kind of mad at the same time, while Emeline was happier than she had ever been in her entire life. They were from two totally opposite ends of the spectrum.

Fiona cleared her throat. "If you wouldn't mind getting him right now, I'll wait here."

Emeline nodded and obediently started to leave but stopped as she reached the door. An unexpected surge of newfound confidence filled her. This woman was obviously here to see Thomas, and the thought of her upsetting the sensitive man she was in love with was unsettling. Clearing her throat, she turned back around to her and spoke with sincerity. "I'm sorry about what happened. But you need to know, he's happy here. This is his home now. It's where he belongs."

Fiona didn't say a word while her fingers tightened around the straps of her handbag in apparent fury. Emeline waited for a response and when she didn't get one, hurried out of the building.

*

As soon as "Annie-get-your-gun" left the gallery, Fiona stomped her foot in anger and took in deep breaths through her nose to keep herself in check. Pacing in the middle of the room under the twinkle lights, her hair caught on one of the fluttering photographs that hung low on the wire. Roughly grabbing it, she eyed it carefully, and a light bulb went off in her head. She looked at another one, and then another before she realized every single picture was of Thomas and Emeline as children and teenagers.

Briskly walking up and down the zigzag display, her blood boiled. How dare this woman interrupt her life and plans, sweeping Thomas off his feet with her pathetic, elementary exhibition of childhood photos? The girl wasn't even a cute child and looked more like a little boy with her flat chest and uneven bangs. Fiona couldn't help herself and started to grab at each photo, pulling them down with a vengeance, her adrenaline pumping with rage. Before she knew it, she was tugging on the wires of the twinkle lights and yanking them down, stomping on the bulbs that crushed into tiny pieces under her heels. For some reason, the impulse to destroy something so thoughtfully romantic brought her much satisfaction.

When she pulled the last wire down from the ceiling and jerked it violently from the wall, sparks shot out of the electrical socket and singed a nearby photo that had floated to the ground. A bead of sweat trickled down her face as she huffed and puffed, taking in the aftermath of her storm. When she heard the hinges of the door squeak, she turned to see Thomas walk through the door and stop. His face expressed bewilderment as he looked around before his heated stare landed on her face.

"Fiona, what have you done?"

His figure was shadowed from the outside sunlight filtering in from behind, his stance large and impressive. Guilt immediately shrouded her in his presence making her feel insignificant, the reality of the mess she had made causing her to recoil.

"I was just leaving," she managed to say between gritted teeth. She picked up her purse she had dropped to the floor, and her heels clicked across the cement floor as she stepped over the tattered photos, wires and broken bulbs. Thomas grabbed her by the arm as she tried to pass.

"Stop it, Fiona! Please. Just—*stop*!"

Her lips trembled as she looked up into his handsome face. His hair was tousled from the sea breeze, and the faint shadow of a beard crossed his chiseled jawline. Emeline was right—he looked happy. He looked like he belonged here. His gorgeous countenance made her feel weak in the knees. He must have sensed her lightheadedness and helped her cross the threshold of the door, holding her by the elbow as he led her outside.

"There's a diner not too far from here. Let's sit and talk there." Fiona could only nod and allowed him to escort her down the street.

As they turned the street corner, a terrible accident was about to unfurl in the gallery. Behind the ancient wall of the electrical outlet, acrid smoke curled through the socket into the space littered with broken lights and precious photos, a leftover ember from Fiona's tantrum. When the spark ignited, flames quickly spread through the sheetrock and up into the ceiling, licking and consuming everything in its path. Lawrence Capshaw's larger-than-life, award-winning photographs hanging on the walls in the iconic gallery fell in giant sheets of impressive flames as the black smoke filled the entire room. The surrounding businesses were oblivious to the horrific scene behind the closed doors until the front glass window exploded and shattered onto the sidewalk from the intense heat inside. Smoke billowed out into the quiet street, alerting nearby pedestrians to the emergency.

Like autumn leaves thrown into a bonfire, photo after photo of Thomas and Emeline curled up and withered in the heat, and soon turned to nothing but ashes on the cement floor. The box with the red lid containing the bulk of pictures from their childhood and teenage summers burned quickly in a tragic display of sparks and flames—decades of precious, tangible memories on film disappearing in the raging inferno in seconds. It was the end of the innocence.

CHAPTER TWENTY- FOUR

Emeline sat at a small table in the coffee house and sipped her beverage while she gazed at the photos she had stashed in her overalls spread out across the table. Her heart was full, and she took her time intensely scrutinizing every picture, the expressions on their youthful faces and the surrounding scenery a small gift from her past. Flipping each photo over, she was impressed that Lawrence Capshaw had hand-written the date, place, and their names in his recognizable cursive writing. The amount of time he had spent on these photos all these years was admirable—a gift of love he had been saving for Thomas and Emeline years later. Fiona Merrill could never compete with memories like this.

When she found Thomas to tell him the news that Fiona was in town and wanted to talk to him at the gallery, he seemed perturbed and promised her he'd take care of it once and for all. Emeline believed him, but still whispered a small prayer that he could convince the intimidating New Yorker to understand, give up and go home.

The sound of sirens made her look out the window just

in time to see a red fire truck whiz by with the lights flashing. It was still pretty early on a Saturday morning, and Emeline was concerned that maybe a tourist had gotten themselves in trouble on the beach. Even though the days were starting to heat up this time of the year, the water was still way too cold to go swimming. With the influx of diehard spring-breakers, they were just crazy enough to jump in, and she hoped it wasn't one of them in distress among the waves and the riptides.

Shoving the photos into her overalls, she stood and grabbed her to-go cup, curiosity getting the better of her. When she stepped outside, the immediate smell of smoke tinged her nostrils and made her eyes water.

"What the...?"

Quickly, she walked the short block to Main Street and turned the corner. The shock that overcame her was instantaneous when she realized the fire truck was parked in front of their gallery fully engulfed in flames. The cup fell from her hands and coffee splattered against her denim overalls and onto the sidewalk. As she bolted like a race horse out of the gates toward the chaos, her legs felt heavy, like she was running in slow motion. A couple of policemen were already on the scene keeping on-lookers and gawkers safely back from the area, the heat oppressive even from a block away.

"*Cappy!*" she screamed, running toward the building. One of the officers grabbed her by the arms and wrestled her back, away from the danger.

"Ma'am, you can't go near there—the building is fully engulfed!" he yelled above the cacophony of noise.

"But my boyfriend is in there! *Oh my god! Thomas is*

inside!" she wailed, flailing in the man's arms.

The fire truck ladder was extended, and streams of water poured out the hose on top of the structure. The ceiling suddenly gave way and collapsed in on itself sending an impressive shower of sparks and flames high into the air, some of them scattering along the street and sidewalks. The officer shielded her for a split second before pushing her into the brick façade of the building they were in front of.

"Stay right here, or you're gonna get yourself killed!" His walkie-talkie was going off with a frantic static message for all units.

Emeline was numb. Her body slowly slid down the side of the building into a heap of despair. As she watched the carnage from afar, her body trembled with the same fear she had experienced the night her mother died. The flames of the gallery reflected in her frightened eyes, and her chest rose and fell in agony knowing that Cappy, the love of her life, was trapped inside.

Clamping her eyes shut, she shook her head and whispered over and over, "This can't be happening. This isn't happening." When she opened her eyes back up, the scene in front of her was too much to bear and looked like something out of a horror movie. Clumsily pushing herself up off the concrete sidewalk with her palms, she gingerly stood and had to catch her balance before a loud moan echoed from her mouth in defeat. After one last agonizing look, she took off running as fast as she could.

***

"I'm sorry about the photos and the lights. I'll pay for the damages," Fiona offered half-heartedly as she sat across from Thomas in the diner.

Picking up his coffee cup, he took a sip and eyed her over the rim. It was unfortunate what Fiona had done in her anger, and as mad as he was at her for destroying his romantic picture display for Emeline, he couldn't blame her after everything that happened. Twinkle lights could be replaced, and the photos could be picked up. But the regret he felt for what he had done to Fiona to advance his career was something he would need to forgive himself for over time.

The wealthy socialite would weather the storm and eventually swindle some other poor schmuck into putting up with her exhausting demands. Hopefully, the guy would be on some different career path other than architecture. What was most concerning was her traveling all the way from New York to Sandersville Beach, a place she swore she would never come to. That she traveled this far to track him down was a bit unnerving.

"What were you trying to accomplish coming here without telling me? Did you want to harass Emeline? Is that why you came?"

Fiona quickly shook her head and wouldn't look him in the eye. "No… I don't know, really. I guess I needed closure. I needed to see it for myself."

"Me and Emeline, together?" he probed, angling his head lower to catch her eye.

When she finally looked up at him, he couldn't help but notice the remorseful look in her blue eyes. "Yes. And it's true. I guess seeing is believing." She offered a half-hearted smirk.

"Well, you came, and you saw. What now?"

Fiona nervously picked up her cup, her vibrant red nails standing out against the white porcelain. After she took a sip, she set it down. "Petra is here with me. I guess we'll go back to New York," she said matter-of-factly.

Thomas nodded. He had seen this reaction before on plenty of occasions. Fiona acted like nothing bothered her, but he knew on the inside, she was hurting. Stretching his hand across the table, he held her fingers. She seemed flustered with his gesture and tried to sit up straighter in her seat. Squeezing her hand, he spoke sincerely. "I'm sorry things didn't work out. You have a beautiful life in New York to go back to with a great group of friends and a father who adores you. I hope you know, I wish you nothing but the best, right?"

Fiona's eyebrow arched in a familiar expression, and she sighed. Pulling her hand from his, she tilted her chin upward. "Thank you, Thomas. I appreciate that."

Sirens could be heard in the distance and the piercing sound continued to get louder. The two of them looked out the giant window at the same time to see a firetruck whiz by with the lights flashing. Thomas furrowed his brow for a second before he turned his attention back to Fiona. She nodded and he watched as she grabbed her purse and stood next to the table. "Don't worry about me. And please, apologize to...whatever her name is—"

"Her name is, Emeline," he interrupted.

Fiona rolled her eyes and said her name with a slight wrinkle to her nose. "Emeline."

Thomas arose from his seat and stood in front of her,

waiting a beat before he opened his arms wide as an act of truce. Sighing, she walked into his embrace and they hugged one last time.

"Goodbye, Thomas," she whispered into his ear before kissing him on the cheek.

Thomas nodded against her blonde hair. "Goodbye, Fiona."

When she pulled back, he noticed her eyes brimmed with tears and her normally resting-bitch-face appeared softer. As she bid one last smile and ran her long nails through the side of his hair, a single tear ran down her cheek before she confidently turned on her high heels and walked out of his life for good.

Thomas sat back down and shook his head in disbelief. What a morning this turned out to be.

"Hey, Thomas. Who was that? Cruella Deville?" Ginger laughed as she refilled his cup of coffee. "Oops, she left a red lip stamp on your cheek. Here, let me get that for you." She pulled a paper napkin from her pocket and ran it up and down his cheek. He felt like a child as he held still for her, amused by her motherly instincts and thankful she hadn't licked the napkin first.

"Thanks, Ginger. It's a long story that Emeline and I will share over dinner sometime." Taking the soiled napkin from her hand, he turned his attention to her and changed the subject. "How are you feeling?"

Ginger rested one hand on her waist. "I'm good. It won't be long now." Turning from side to side, she humorously showed off her bulging profile.

Thomas nodded with pleasure. Ginger and Rusty McCormick were going to be great friends, he was sure of it. The next chapter in their lives loomed on the horizon and filled him with great happiness. "You're mighty close to that due date. Don't overdo it."

"Yes, sir," she teased. "Do you want to see a menu?"

"No, thanks. I'm meeting Emmy back at the gallery. Can I get two cups of coffee to go? One with two sugars, the other with cream."

"Coming right up." She smiled and waddled off.

Stretching his neck from side to side, he inhaled deeply, thankful that the morning wasn't completely ruined. He couldn't wait to speak with Emeline about her encounter with Fiona and hoped she wasn't too shocked by the woman's unexpected arrival. What a cluster-fuck.

With coffee finally in hand, he resumed what should have been his earlier routine. They had a lot to accomplish today and were now behind schedule. When he stepped outside the diner, he was immediately hit with the smell of something burning. Concerned etched his face as he remembered the fire truck speeding by, and he walked briskly through town toward Main Street. A barricade had been put up at the far end of the road, closing it off, and a crowd of people were gawking and pointing at plumes of black smoke rising into the sky. Curious, Thomas edged his way toward the front of the group, and his mouth dropped, along with the two coffees. Ducking under the sawhorse brackets, an officer tried to stop him.

"*Sir*! You can't go down there! The building is on fire!"

Disregarding the officer's warning, he sprinted past

him, his concern for Emeline the only thing on his mind. His lungs burned the closer he got before he was abruptly halted by Rusty McCormick dressed in head to toe fire gear.

"*Thomas*!" he shouted. But Thomas couldn't respond, the fear paralyzing him in his stance as he tried to catch his breath and watched the structure burn fearing Emmy was inside. "Thomas, buddy! Where're doing everything can. You gotta move back. It's too dangerous!"

The fire had spread to two other galleries in the Pineapple Grove district, his grandfather's burning completely out of control, the billowing smoke rising high in the caustic air. There was no way anyone could survive a fire that intense.

"*Emeline*!" he managed to shout above the chaotic noise, his head dizzy from the smoke and all the commotion.

"The building is all clear!" Rusty yelled, focused on Thomas as if trying to read him. When Thomas didn't respond, he gripped him firmly by both arms and repeated himself. "Did you hear me? The building is all clear! No one is inside!"

"Emeline is in there!" Thomas cried desperately.

Rusty shook his head vigorously. "No, man! There wasn't anyone inside. I can promise you that!"

Thomas's breathing accelerated with the joyous news, and he snapped out of his shocked daze, forcefully gripping Rusty by the arms. "Are you fucking sure?"

"Yes!" he shouted, pushing him toward safety. "Get

out of here and go find her. It's all good, man!"

Thomas stumbled to the curb, not knowing where to go. And then it hit him—an image of Emeline's painting coming to mind.

"*Run to the Sea*," he whispered hoarsely to himself. His heart leaped with elation knowing exactly where Emeline was, and he took off like a jack-rabbit, running as if his life depended on it.

CHAPTER TWENTY-FIVE

The buildings and palm trees were a blur to Thomas as he sprinted through town toward the ocean. His heart pounded, and he gasped for sweet air as he pushed himself faster and faster, running at full speed. When he got close to the pier, his feet slid out from under him when he hit the sand-scattered pavement that edged the first dune next to the weathered planks. Catching his balance, he gasped for air and searched the long stretch of wood that jutted out over the water. A few lone fishermen were casting their reels among the roar of the surf, and a couple with a camera took pictures. Thomas jogged across the planks, shielding his eyes from the intense glare of the sun, hoping Emmy was sitting on one of the built-in benches. When he didn't see her, he scanned the north shore and frantically yelled her name into the sea breeze.

"*Emeline!*"

Tourists were already camped out on fabric beach chairs and towels along the sandy shore under colorful umbrellas spiked into the sand. Several teens were daring each other into the frigid blue water, and the seagulls called out as they hovered in a small flock over a child happily tossing food into the air. His pulse continued to hammer as his eyes darted from one group to the next. Turning toward the southside, he scanned the beach and noticed a lone figure in denim sitting close to the water. There was no towel or chair to speak of, and her long, russet hair blew haphazardly in the wind as she clutched her knees to her chest. His heart pumped fervently, knowing it was Emeline. Cupping his hands on both sides of his mouth, he yelled as loud as he could.

"*Emeline!*"

He watched as she turned her head in recognition and his breathing staggered as he bit his lip to keep from bursting into tears. She struggled to stand, and her face tilted upward as if searching the pier for the person calling out to her.

"*Emeline! I'm here! I'm here, Emmy!*" he screamed.

She darted too quickly toward the pier and stumbled, sending a spray of sand all around her. Swiftly, she got back up and started to run. The sound of his name was music to his ears as she screamed from the top of her lungs. "*Cappy! Cappy!*"

A smile erupted across his face sending a burst of strength through his body, and his feet pounded the wooden planks as he rushed to get to her. When he reached the beach, he forged ahead faster and faster, his sole focus on the love of his life running toward him. She flung her body into his arms, and he twirled her around with elation. Clinging to each other, he was desperate to know what happened and took in big gulps of air, finding it difficult to form words on his lips.

"Are you all right? Are you hurt?" He touched her face and her mouth, anxious for a response, yet pleased to feel her in his arms.

Her lashes were wet with tears, and her lips trembled. "I…I thought I lost you," she heaved.

Thomas shook his head and held her cheek tenderly in his hand. "Never. You'll never lose me, Emmy. Never, *ever.*"

Consumed with euphoria, he pressed his fevered lips against hers, and they kissed passionately as the warm, salty air swirled around them. As the kiss intensified, Thomas kept his eyes shut tightly to thwart off the sudden onset of emotions he was feeling. A sob bubbled up from the depths of his soul, and their lips disengaged as he pulled her tightly into his torso, the wail of pure relief overwhelming him as he shuddered, his emotions on full display. Her shoulders shook as they wept in each other's arms, the enormity of what happened a sobering reality.

"How did you know where to find me?" Her sweet voice seemed calmer after their emotional outburst, and she pulled back from him, brushing her knuckles across her wet cheek.

Thomas licked his lips and nodded. "Your painting. I just…knew."

Emeline stared back at him with wide, amber eyes and nodded. "I waited for you. I prayed, and I hoped beyond hope that you weren't in there…I was in the coffee shop around the corner. When I went back to the gallery, it was already on fire. I thought you were inside…I thought I lost you in that fire…" Her breath hitched, and she started to sob again, hiding her face against his chest.

"Shh, I'm here, Emmy. I'm here. I wasn't in the gallery. I was still at the diner. I'm here now. I'm not going anywhere," he soothed.

Squinting up into the cloudless blue sky, he held her close and sighed with relief. The realization of losing his grandfather's gallery was heartbreaking after everything they had been through. But the idea of losing Emeline was even more traumatic. Just as his grandfather had communicated through his photography where Thomas belonged, Emmy had communicated her safe place through her painting. It was remarkable, really—hidden messages from the two people who meant more to him than anything.

Taking her by the hand, they slowly trudged through the heavy sand toward the pier, their connection suddenly on a much deeper level. It was beautifully basic, yet painfully meaningful—the hidden truths of their lives unexpectedly revealed through penetrating loss and heartache.

***

Fiona sat on the edge of the king-sized hotel bed fixated on the television screen in front of her while she stared at the images of the Lawrence Capshaw Gallery on the local news channel. It was nothing but a pile of burned rubble. Not two hours ago, she was standing in that same building that was now burned to the ground. Her mouth was agape, and she was so tuned in to whatever the newscaster was saying that she didn't hear Petra come in.

"*Fiona!*" She harped, startling her.

"*What?*" Fiona glared at her friend and turned the

sound down with the remote before realizing she had overreacted. "You scared me, Petra. What is it?"

Petra stood in the doorway with her arms crossed against her chest, eyeing her curiously. She was wearing a crocheted cover-up over her swimsuit, and her expensive sunglasses were perched high on her head, holding back her jet-black hair. "What is so mesmerizing on the TV? Huh? This weather is gorgeous. We have one glorious afternoon on the beach before we have to head back home. Are you coming or not?"

Fiona waved her off. "I'll be there soon. Promise."

Petra shrugged, turned and left. Fiona immediately turned the volume back up and continued to listen to the breaking news story as she nervously fiddled with her long fingernails. The commentator mentioned something about an electrical fire that started the blaze in the photography gallery. She wondered...could this have been her fault? Did she cause this? She vaguely remembered seeing sparks when she violently pulled a strand of cheap lights from the electrical socket during her rage after seeing photos of Thomas and Emeline together.

Biting her lower lip, her eyes grew large when a crew went live at the scene, and none other than Thomas Capshaw himself filled the entire screen. As the news reporter asked him questions, Fiona couldn't help but swoon thinking Thomas looked handsome as ever, even in his depressed state. Her eyebrow cocked with interest as she leaned forward to concentrate on the interview.

"The cause of the fire is still under investigation, but the Fire Chief told us earlier it may have started because of an electrical issue. Were you aware of any problems in the building?"

Thomas shook his head. "No. I mean, I know this part of Sandersville Beach is older, and some of the buildings haven't been updated in quite some time. I'm sure we'll know more once the investigation is complete."

"The loss of art to this community is devastating, the damage to at least two other studios significant. Your late grandfather was renowned photographer, Lawrence Capshaw, an icon in this community. We've learned his estate was recently settled. Were you able to get most of his famous photographs out before the fire?"

"Yes," Thomas nodded. "His entire office was recently cleaned out, and we have original proofs and negatives of all his award-winning photographs safely off-site."

"That's good to hear. Was there anything of sentimental value that you lost in the fire? Anything you wish you could have gotten out before this happened?"

Fiona watched as Thomas sighed with downcast eyes.

"There was a box of personal photographs that we lost."

"Oh, I'm so sorry to hear that. Photographs of your family?"

Thomas nodded. "Yes. They were very dear to me, and I'm hoping there are negatives somewhere that weren't destroyed."

Fiona recalled the photographs fluttering romantically in the space. Knowing these were the obliterated pictures destroyed by fire that Thomas referenced left her with a peculiar sense of deep satisfaction. What was wrong with her? Shouldn't she be sympathetic to his loss? Was she really that horrible and selfish of a person? As she listened to Thomas ramble about what a good job the fire department did and how grateful he was no one was hurt, she stood, pressed her fingertips to her lips and placed her hand on the screen reflecting Thomas's image.

"*Au revoir*," she said out loud before she turned the television off with one click. If she was a horrible person, then so was Thomas Capshaw after what he did behind her back with her own father.

Grabbing her swimsuit out of a drawer, she smiled to herself and energetically shouted through the doorway into the hotel sitting room, "I'm on my way, Petra!" The guilt was short-lived as a strange sense of fulfillment overcame her, knowing Thomas had lost something special too.

Now they were even.

CHAPTER TWENTY-SIX

"Order up, Em!" Harold called out from behind the kitchen counter.

Emeline quickly grabbed a tray and loaded it up with an assortment of hearty breakfast platters ordered by a large group of spring break frat boys. When she passed them out efficiently to each hungry guy, they acted like ravenous wild animals and immediately dug in like they hadn't eaten for days. She paused and watched them in awe, her smile wide.

"I'll bring over another pitcher of coffee and soda."

A couple of grunts were offered before she left the table to fetch a clean pitcher. As she loaded it with ice and held it under the cola spout to fill it up, Ginger waddled over to her.

"It's insane this morning," she complained.

"Tell me about it," Emeline replied, resting one hand on her hip. The diner was bustling with loud conversation and held a certain indefinable spirit that made her feel at home.

"How long is spring break anyway?"

"Depends on the county. It usually falls in the month of April. They're right on time."

"Hmmm," Ginger contemplated. "If I can make another couple days of this chaos, I'm home free for baby girl."

"How is she today?" Emeline asked, smiling at her friend.

Ginger rubbed her belly that seemed to be getting bigger by the minute. "She's rambunctious!"

The two girls giggled before Ginger lowered her voice. "How are you holding up? Rusty said he talked to you a couple of nights ago to confirm the fire was electrical. Have y'all decided what you're going to do?"

Emeline sighed. The tragedy of what happened was a major setback in her and Thomas's plans. For the first twenty-four hours after the fire, she had an unrealistic fear that he would throw in the towel, pack his bags and go back to his steady job in New York. Thomas assured her that would never, *ever* happen—that his life was in Sandersville Beach, with her. Still, her angst was real, and her dreams of seeing her artwork on display in a real gallery showing were shelved indefinitely.

"He's talking to someone about buying out the lease and owning the property outright."

"Isn't that expensive?"

"I don't know. He says he has an idea to redesign an even better space and help rebuild the block."

"Well, that's amazing news! I guess being an architect has come in handy," Ginger animatedly expressed. "I'm just so glad you and Thomas weren't in there when it happened. Rusty said all of Pineapple Grove could have gone up in flames if their response time had been even a few minutes later."

Emeline exhaled a breath of air slowly and nodded. Ginger was right—it could have been a lot worse. But dammit, it didn't have to happen at all either. Not wanting to upset Thomas, she kept a positive outlook and reassured him everything was fine even though she was devastated on the inside. She knew it was petty, but the setback of not having the gallery anymore for her own showing left her feeling sad, and she wondered if it wasn't meant to be. Was she even good enough? Or was she riding on his name to get her foot in the door? And then there was the matter of Fiona Merrill being in town the very same day the fire happened. What were the chances of that? The memories of that odd, serendipitous day made her shudder—especially during that small window of time when she thought she had lost him.

Emeline offered Ginger a small smile. "Like Thomas says, we'll rebuild, and it will be better than ever."

Ginger reached out and touched her arm in support. "It will. And the best part about it is you're together."

Riding her bike back through town after her shift at the diner, Emeline couldn't help herself and peddled down Main Street where she stopped in front of the burned rubble of what was once Lawrence Capshaw's photography gallery. The faint scent of charred wood lingered in the ocean breeze as she sadly scanned the massive path of destruction blocked off with yellow hazard tape.

What really gutted her was losing the box of photos— the hundreds and hundreds of memories chronicling her life with Thomas. It was a massive loss for both of them.

Closing her eyes to thwart her pain, she thought about the last time she stood in the gallery space looking at the photos he had so lovingly arranged clipped onto the crisscrossed wires of the twinkle lights. She would never forget that night and the surprise he had so painstakingly arranged just for her. The memory brought a smile to her face before she suddenly inhaled and opened her eyes wide as a different memory surfaced.

Clumsily, she got back on her bike and turned toward the ocean. Why in the past few days hadn't she remembered this before? Her heart raced with gladness, her feet barely keeping up with the circular motion of the fast-moving pedals as she raced toward Cap Cottage.

***

Thomas paced the weathered deck of his new home with his cell phone pressed to his ear and listened to his mother go over a checklist of things to ask the insurance adjustor and the building owners.

"I'm already on it, Mom," he reassured her. "I can't believe this made national news. I guess that proves how important Pop was in the art world."

Scanning the ocean with his free hand on his hip, he sighed at her reply. "I know. I'm sad too, but we talked about this. If I can make this deal happen, we'll rebuild something even better, and you can come down for the grand re-opening. Sound good?"

He listened as his mother told him she'd help in any way possible to honor her father and would be there with bells on. "Okay," he chuckled. "I gotta go. I'll call you in a few days with an update. I love you, Mom." He couldn't help but smile when she told him she loved him too.

Clicking off his phone with a sigh, he shoved it into his board shorts and looked out over the surface of the water. The view from Cap Cottage was something he would never grow tired of. The ocean went on forever—it was infinite, pure and mysterious, full of life and death swirling together in a beautiful dance. This was his home now, with Emeline. This was where he had always belonged.

They had moved all her things out of her garage apartment and into the beach home, including her numerous art supplies and paintings that were stacked upright in his boyhood bedroom. Thank god they hadn't taken them to the gallery yet, the thought of all her hard work going up in flames a dismal notion.

While mapping out his plan for his next steps, he knew he wanted to marry her. Thinking back to that first night he discovered his grandmother's ring amidst the box of photos, he was thankful he had good enough sense to pull it from the box and stash it in a safe place at Cap Cottage. If it had been lost in the fire, he would have never forgiven himself. Knowing it was out of harm's way brought him much needed peace after everything that had happened. The anticipation of placing it on Emeline's finger would finally be the beginning of their happily ever after.

A door slammed, and Thomas turned to peer into the

cottage, half-expecting Emeline to come out and greet him after her shift at the diner. When she didn't, he called out to her.

"Emmy? Are you home?" The French doors creaked as he reentered the house. He could hear more noises and shuffling coming from the master bedroom. "Em? What are you doing?"

Standing next to their closet, she had pulled out the dirty clothes hamper and was frantically grabbing items and tossing them about. "I remembered something." Her voice cracked with emotion as she pulled her dirty overalls from the very bottom of the hamper and sat on the floor, still dressed in her waitress uniform.

Thomas frowned and squatted across from her, eyeing her with concern. "What did you remember?"

Her bosom rose and fell as she took in deep breaths and looked at him with wide-eyed anticipation as she gripped the clothing in her hands. Biting her lower lip, she dipped her hand into the front chest pocket of the overalls and pulled out a handful of photos. Pure elation crossed her features, and she started to laugh and cry at the same time.

"Emmy? What is it? What's happening?" Quickly, he scooted across the wooden floor and folded her in his arms as she clasped her hands against her chest. "Please, tell me what's wrong."

"Nothing is wrong," she cried, smiling through her tears. "I was pulling our pictures off the twinkle lights and kept a few of my favorites to bring home to put on the refrigerator." She brought her hands down and fanned the photos in front of her like a deck of cards to show him. "I completely forgot about putting them in my pocket after the fire happened."

Thomas stared at the familiar photos in awe, the images of a much younger version of themselves smiling back at them through time. His grandfather's tiny cursive writing comforted him in the moment. It was an unexpected gift, and he couldn't help but reach out and lightly touch the corner of one of the pictures as if to make sure it was real.

"I rode by the gallery on my way home, and it suddenly dawned on me. I got here as fast as I could." She started to laugh again. "Thank god you didn't start the laundry today."

Thomas let out a chuckle before he shook his head, amazed at this simple, amazing, wonderful gift. All was not lost, the photos in Emmy's hand proof of that. It was as if his grandfather had reached out to him yet again from afar, reminding him of what he deserved after all this time. He couldn't help but recall that last conversation he ever had with Pop, when he called in a last-ditch effort telling him point blank that he deserved love, not prestige—that being a part of the Merrill family was not his destiny. How right he was. As he held his love in his arms, they reminisced about their past in the faded photos, and he couldn't help but look forward to their future, his grandmother's ring on the forefront of his mind.

CHAPTER TWENTY-SEVEN

The morning light came in through the windows, casting beams of warmth over the tops of Emeline's toes as she sat on her stool and painted. This was her favorite time of day at Cap Cottage. When she first moved in while Thomas was still in New York, she stumbled upon this romantic hour when she came out of the bedroom half-asleep forging for a cup of water. The morning light stopped her in her tracks, and she ended up painting through the first half of the day in her pajamas.

Dressed in nothing but a bathrobe, she quietly mixed a dab of Alizarin Crimson with a touch of Titanium White on her palette to try to match the sweeping pinks of the sunrise where the water kissed the sky. The canvas in front of her was a new project, and she was going outside her comfort zone using more color—happier colors. It wasn't that her old artwork was colorless, it was just—darker.

Thomas seemed to love her work in progress, and if she were up early painting, he would quietly enter the room and kiss her cheek, offer a heartfelt, "good morning," fetch a cup of coffee and leave her be. In the past, when she lived in her old apartment, she often packed up a smaller version of her art supplies and walked to the beach to play with the colors and the light near the ocean. Now that she had a front-row seat to Mother Nature, the inspiration was endless, which made her a blissful girl.

A pod of dolphins popped up every few feet in their quest north, and Emeline paused, still holding her brush, to stare out at the calm water as their fins sent ripples across the glassy surface. Gentle waves came ashore to the secluded beach and she couldn't help but feel blessed as an audience of one witnessing the brilliance that was the Sandersville Beach coastline. She had to admit, her new home was a long way from the dingy garage apartment she could barely afford. Thomas had changed all of that. It was odd feeling the same fluttering of her heart she remembered from her youth every time he was around. Even with the expanse of time and distance, and the past mistakes they had both made, they seemed to pick up right where they left off, only on a much deeper level. When she told him she loved him, she meant it. He was the love of her life since day one.

The sun moved slowly up her bare legs as she resumed her painting. Using an overlapping sweeping motion with her flat brush loaded with the replicated pink color of the morning sky, she diluted it with water. Her technique created a natural fade, helping to differentiate the separation of sea and sky. No matter how careful she was while creating, she always managed to splatter herself with some form of color. Her fingertips were already pink, and the edge of her hand was smeared with her sunset creation from concentrating too hard while up close to the canvas. No matter, the acrylic paint was easy to wash off, although there were times she enjoyed wearing the paint splatters like a badge of creative honor in the artistic town.

"Good morning," Thomas whispered, bending over and kissing her on top of the head like clock-work. She hadn't heard him walk into the room and took a deep breath to come back to the present.

"Good morning," she replied happily. Glancing at his backside dressed in loose-fitting sweatpants, she couldn't help the sly smile that graced her lips. Shirtless and with messy bed-head hair, he was the epitome of the perfect boyfriend, especially with his scruffy cheeks and chin. Distracted by his undeniable good looks, her eyes darted back and forth from her painting to his pecs. He poured himself a cup of coffee, grabbed his notebook from the side table, and went out to the large deck, being careful not to obscure her morning view.

Emeline sighed contentedly, thankful she was finally living her best life filled with beauty, art, and love. It was a far cry from her home life growing up. If Lawrence Capshaw were still alive, he'd be clicking away on his camera taking pictures of the two of them as they navigated this new chapter in their lives as best friends and lovers. Glancing at the photos she saved from the gallery tacked onto the refrigerator, she smiled as an idea formed. Licking her lips, she set her brush down and stood.

Thomas was covered in the golden morning light, his focus on a sketch in his notebook. Emeline stared for a moment, her heart aching with unmistakable love. He must have felt her presence because he stopped and looked over at her.

"Finished already?" His smile in the romantic light made his eyes sparkle like precious blue jewels as he closed his notebook and gave her his full attention.

"Yeah," she replied inching herself closer to him. He held out his hand, and she took it. "I had an idea."

"Oh? What is it?" He patted his thigh where she nestled on his lap and wrapped her arms around his neck.

"Do you still have any of Pop's cameras?"

Thomas thought for a moment. "I'm sure I saw a couple in the closet where he left some of my sketchbooks. Why do you ask?"

"I want us to use one of them—to take some pictures."

"Okay? Why do you want to take pictures, Emmy?" Bringing his hand up to her face, he gently pushed her hair over her shoulder, his fingers lingering on her bare neck.

"Well, when we were growing up, he was always taking pictures of us. If he were here today, I think he'd still be taking pictures—of us."

"So, you want to take pictures—of us?"

"Something like that," she giggled, aware that what she was saying probably wasn't making much sense.

Thomas caressed her chin and lightly ran his index finger across her bottom lip, causing her lower region to melt with heat.

"Emmy, you're so beautiful in this light. I'd love a picture of you just like this." He paused and traced her face as if he were planning a sketch. "Do you know how hard it is for me not to bother you on the mornings you like to paint? Especially knowing you're naked under your bathrobe?"

Emeline pursed her lips and slowly shook her head, never taking her gaze off Thomas's compelling blue eyes. His hand slid down her neck, and he paused before gripping the lapel of her robe and pulling it off her shoulder.

"Cappy…" she murmured as her breast was revealed and the light morning breeze floated over the top of her erect nipple. Her breath hitched, and she shifted, stretching her neck forward to kiss his lips while palming the hard planes of his bare chest. The warm, coffee-flavored tip of his tongue slipped through the seam of her mouth and teased her while he massaged her with his hand. The robe fell further off her shoulder, and he pushed it to the side, her naked body writhing on his lap. She could feel his hardness through his sweatpants and knew he wasn't wearing any underwear.

"Straddle me, Emmy," he whispered wantonly, gripping her by the hips and helping her shift into the new position. Using both hands, he aggressively shoved the robe off her until she was completely naked on top of him in the chair.

Her chest heaved as she languished in the pleasure he was giving. Reaching between his legs, she dipped her hands over the waistband of his pants and freed his engorged manhood from the fabric. Her wet seam throbbed with want, and she pulled back from him, eagerly massaging his hot skin.

"You want it out here? For the entire world to see?" she teased aggressively.

His mouth was open as he hungrily looked at her, pulsing to the rhythm she created with her hands. "Oh, yes. Right now, Em."

"But what if someone sees us?" She giggled naughtily.

Thomas leaned forward and raked his teeth over her nipple. "Believe me, no one is on the beach this early."

Lifting herself slightly off his thighs, she slowly positioned her wet core over his stiffness. The explicit pleasure that coursed through her body as she eased herself onto him was immediate, and she couldn't help but moan.

"Oh, god yes…" Thomas mumbled, holding her steady on top of him. The slow, rolling movement they fell in to was beautiful—unhurried and firm, focused and intentional among the amazing backdrop of the magnificent ocean. She could honestly say she felt like the goddess of love and beauty in Botticelli's painting, The Birth of Venus, born of the sea spray and blown there by the winds.

It wasn't until Thomas grabbed her long hair by the nape and tilted her neck back so she looked up into the endless sky, that her orgasm mounted, and she felt like she was flying high among the clouds. The pain was exquisite, and she tried to hold back as Thomas thrust harder.

"Let go, sweet Emmy," he rumbled in her ear before possessively clamping his mouth over hers.

Emeline compressed her eyes and concentrated on the delicious friction between their bodies, her orgasm building with intensity. When she hit the top of the cliff and started free falling into space, her back arched, and she gripped Thomas by the shoulders shuddering with release. The orgasm was so intense, her eyes rolled back, and she had to remember to breathe for fear of passing out from the bliss. Thomas soon followed and gasped, bucking underneath her in sweet freedom. When they finally came down, she laid her head in the crevice of his neck and nuzzled him.

"I love you," he managed to say between staggered breaths while stroking her hair away from her blushing skin.

"I love you too, Cappy."

Closing her heavy eyelids, she could feel him stretch and ease the robe over her shoulders again, shielding her nakedness from the outdoors. As he held her in his arms, she sleepily opened one eye and watched with fascination as the pink sky faded into the first blue hues of a gorgeous day.

CHAPTER TWENTY-EIGHT

"Oh, my goodness, Ginger! She's so little." Emeline watched with fascination as the hospital nurse handed Ginger a tiny baby swaddled in a pink blanket. Crossing the room, she sat on the edge of the bed and gazed at her friend's beautiful newborn daughter. "Have you and Rusty decided on a name yet?"

"No," Rusty bellowed humorously as he entered the room making everyone laugh. "I have my favorites, and she has hers. We decided to take a poll with everyone who visits."

Ginger nudged her with her elbow. "His favorites remind me of 1940s pinup girls—Mabel, Ava, Ruby…"

"Well what about yours, darlin'? You picked names from your favorite shows from the 90s—Carrie, Samantha, Charlotte, Miranda…"

"Ginger! You didn't!" Emeline laughed.

Ginger rolled her eyes. "He's teasing, Emmy. I put those names on my list as a joke, and he won't let me forget it."

By this time, Rusty was on the other side of the bed near his wife and new daughter. Emeline watched as he lovingly cupped the top of his newborn's head and leaned his large frame lower to kiss Ginger tenderly on the mouth. Their little family was precious, and she couldn't help but put her hand over her heart and smile.

"You should have seen her, Emeline. Ginger was a champ."

"Oh, I don't know about that. It hurt like the dickens!"

"She nearly squeezed my hand off when she was pushing. Nearly stopped the blood flow to my fingers," he laughed.

Ginger giggled and turned toward Emeline, holding her bundle of joy out for her. "Here Emmy. Hold baby girl for a minute while Rusty helps me to the ladies' room."

Emeline had never held a baby before and immediately stiffened as she took the baby burrito from Ginger's arms.

"Just keep her little head steady, and you'll be fine," she reassured.

Staring into the little girl's face, Emeline was taken aback by how tiny her features were. Her skin was amazingly soft as she lightly stroked her flawless cheek, and her button nose reminded her of Ginger's. Tiny, dark eyelashes fanned out from her closed eyes as she slept, her rosebud lips occasionally sucking the air. The small human enthralled Emeline, and for a brief second, she wondered what it would be like to be a mother to her own child someday.

Rusty lovingly helped Ginger back into the bed and

pulled up a chair next to her. They chatted for several more minutes until the infant started to squirm, indicating feeding time. Handing off "baby girl" to her mother, Emeline stepped back and sighed at the happy, domestic scene.

"Congratulations, both of you," she offered whole-heartedly.

"Thank you," they said in unison.

"Hopefully, you and Thomas will be next, and baby girl will have a best friend to grow up with," Ginger gleefully insisted. When she casually lifted the edge of her hospital gown and exposed her engorged tit to breastfeed her baby, Emeline's eyes grew large at the sight and quickly bid them farewell, making the happy couple roll with laughter.

Walking down the long hospital corridor toward the lobby, Emeline couldn't help but wonder if babies were in the cards for them. Wouldn't it be something if she and Thomas had a child that could be friends with Rusty and Ginger's daughter while growing up together? She sighed at the thought as she pushed open the double glass doors and exited into the bright sunshine.

***

"Cappy? Are you here?"

Thomas could hear Emeline in the house over the roar of the surf. His hair was mussed from the breeze, and he patted it down as he went inside. "I'm here. How's Ginger? Did you hold the baby?"

Emeline smiled, and he noticed her face dotted with color from her bike ride back to the cottage. "Ginger is

Superwoman, Rusty is Superman and baby girl is adorable…"

Thomas chuckled. "Let me guess—they still haven't agreed on a name?"

Emeline shook her head and grinned. "Nope."

"Come here," he requested, opening his arms wide for a hug. When she was nestled against his chest, he groaned with relief. "Mmmmm. Sorry I couldn't go with you today."

"No worries. You'll see them when we take dinner over to their place tomorrow," she said, pulling back from him. "How was the meeting with the owners? Did you settle on a price? Are they moving forward with the sale?"

Thomas raked his top teeth over his bottom lip, not yet ready to tell her his news. "Come," he said, holding out his hand for her to take. "We can talk on the beach."

Emeline's brow creased with worry as she took his hand and followed him outside. They walked down the old wooden walkway across the dunes and sawgrass to a familiar stretch of sand and continued to a spot that Thomas had set up with a large blanket spread out next to a picnic basket. Her eyes lit up at the sight.

"Cappy? What have you done?"

Thomas led her to the blanket edge and helped lower her to the fabric. He sat next to her and stretched his legs out before grabbing the basket and pulling out a small plate holding assorted cheeses, crackers, and plump, purple grapes. Emeline giggled with delight as the ocean breeze blew tiny tendrils of hair that had fallen out of her ponytail around her face. They often enjoyed happy hour on the sand while watching the light change into dusk.

"For you." He happily handed her a stem-less wineglass before reaching in the basket and grabbing the bottle of white wine he had chilled earlier. He poured the faint yellow liquid into their glasses and held his up in the air toward hers. "I want to make a toast."

Emmy stared back at him with warm eyes and smiled demurely. "What are we celebrating, Cappy? Can you please tell me now?"

He nodded and cleared his throat. "Cheers to the new owners of Capshaw Galleries…" Before he could finish, Emeline was squealing with delight and grabbed the back of his neck with her free hand pulling him into her mouth for a wet kiss.

"*Woah*! Emmy! I don't want to spill this all over you…"

"Oh, my god, Cappy! That's great news! I'm so proud of you!" Her enthusiasm was infectious, and he couldn't help but grin from ear to ear.

"The plot is ours, Emmy. I've got the plans for the new build and the contractors already lined up. It's going to be amazing. Here, let me show you." Pulling a notebook from the basket, he showed her a rough sketch of his plans. As she looked on with interest, he couldn't help but notice the firm grip of her hand on his bicep and the way her face displayed pleasure at what he was showing her. His heart started to speed up, knowing he was about to show her something even better.

"There's one more thing."

"What?" she asked, taking a sip of wine. He noticed she had slipped off her shoes and was rubbing her feet together in the sand, her toenail polish the same blue-green color from her painting hanging in the home they shared together.

"I need you to look through some other ideas I had— to make sure this is a go."

"Oh. Okay." Licking her lips, she set her glass down on the blanket, and he handed her the notebook.

"Just flip through the pages and tell me what you think."

Nodding happily, she adjusted the book on her lap and looked down at the first page. Her smile faded as she turned the page, and her chest started to heave after several more pages. Looking up at him, she looked like she was about to cry.

"Keep going," Thomas gently insisted while watching her every move.

The notebook contained different sketches he had drawn of Emeline over the years they grew up together taped to the pages. Some of them were on sheets of paper, others were on napkins or on the backs of receipts— anything he could find at the time in his young life to draw on. Knowing how upset she had been losing the box of photos in the fire, he decided to pull out the stored boxes of sketch pads his grandfather had saved in his boyhood closet. It was a treasure chest of memories, and he knew it would be something meaningful to her, especially on a day like today.

"Cappy, I... I can't believe you found all of these and

put this together for me. When did you…?"

"Shhh. Keep going. I need you to get to the end." In addition to the sketches from his youth, he added recent sketches he had drawn since they had reunited.

Biting her lip to stifle a smile, she nodded and kept turning the pages. The early evening sky started to change color, the blue slowly replaced with an infusion of vibrant orange and lavender. The glow to her skin was magical, and the air was filled with energy. A few evening strollers walked by, leaving footprints in the sand as Emeline continued to flip through the notebook, taking her time with each page. Occasionally, she would emit a sudden gasp or a little, "oh," and her eyes misted the more she took it all in as if she were watching a film reel of their life together—and it kind of was.

In his youth, Thomas had taken the cue from his grandfather, noticing everyone and everything around him, sketching the world and the details as he saw it, through his own lens—his eyes and fingers. Much of that world included Emeline.

He knew she was coming to the end when he spotted the sketch of her sleeping he had done earlier in the week. And when she turned to the last page, her face scrunched in confusion, and she turned to look at him.

"A question mark?" she asked, closing the book.

"Mhmm," Thomas uttered, aware that his hands were starting to shake.

"What's the question, Cappy?"

Thomas took a deep breath and reached for her hand.

"I love you, Emmy."

"I love you too, Cappy."

"I'm so glad, Em. I'm so glad we've reunited after all these years. My life has changed so much in such a short time—for the better."

"Mine too."

He nodded. "Things have also changed with the gallery—for the better. To own it outright is the best thing for us. But I don't think I can do it alone. I need a partner…"

Emeline's face fell, and she looked away from him, as if embarrassed. "Cappy, you know I don't have any savings or bonds or…."

"I'm not talking about a financial partner," he interrupted. When she finally looked back up at him, he continued. "I'm talking about a *life* partner." Dipping his fingers into his jeans pocket, he pulled out his grandmother's ring and held it up into the light, making Emeline gasp.

"My grandfather knew from day one that you were the girl for me. We were best friends growing up, and I thought you'd be in my life forever. I inherited this ring when my grandmother died, but I was very young, and Pop knew better than to give it to a kid. He held on to it all these years but never told me where he put it."

Emeline hung on his every word as the facets of the diamond glimmered in the softening glow of the sky.

"I thought it was lost until I came back to Sandersville

Beach and ran into you again. And then you offered to help me clean out his studio, and we found the box with the red lid—all the photos he had saved of you and me… To be reunited with my *best friend* is the greatest thing that has ever happened to me." By this time, Thomas's emotions were threatening to surface, and he had to stop and wipe a rogue tear that spilled from the corner of his eye.

"Oh, don't cry, Cappy," she soothed, cupping his face with her hand.

"Emmy, the ring was in the box of photos. He was waiting for me to give it to you. He wanted me to marry *you*. He knew all this time, and I think I did too, but we were so young, and I was stupid not to answer your letters…"

Pausing, he allowed Emeline to wipe his face and stared poignantly into her warm, amber gaze. "Will you, Em? Will you be my partner—my best friend forever?" His voice caught in his throat, and he held his breath as he shifted to one knee and presented her with the ring. "Will you marry me?"

When she nodded without hesitation, he placed the diamond on her finger and brought her hand up to his mouth to kiss. Their eyes were glued to each other for several seconds before they lunged at the same time and hugged. Holding her tightly in his arms, the love he felt for this woman, his Emmy, was real, and the warmth in his heart spilled over into his entire being like the amber light from her eyes.

It was a full-circle moment, and the past was finally behind them. The future was limitless with Emeline by his side. This was where he was destined to be—right here on

Sandersville Beach with his best friend in his arms.

Thomas Capshaw was finally home.

THE END

THOMAS & EMELINE'S PLAYLIST

Here are a few favorite songs that inspired my writing –

One Tree Hill – U2
Best Shot – Jimmie Allen
Speechless – Dan & Shay
In My blood – Shawn Mendes
Life and Death – Paul Cardall
I Like Me Better – Lauv
Delicate – Taylor Swift
What Happens In A Small Town – Brantley Gilbert
Lovers In Japan – Coldplay
Pictures of You – The Cure
A Thousand Years – Christina Perri
Free – Zac Brown Band
All We'd Ever Need – Lady Antebellum
The Breaker – Little Big Town
Summer Wind – Frank Sinatra
Pieces – Red
The End of the Innocence – Don Henley

Enjoy these tunes on the exclusive *Run to the Sea* SPOTIFY playlist! https://goo.gl/jPeKgK

For more music and inspiration, check out my website:
www.kgfletcherauthor.com

ACKNOWLEDGEMENTS

I can remember exactly where I was when the idea came to me to write this new series. I was with my band on tour waiting outside for our rental van in the freezing cold last fall. I kept thinking to myself how I would love to be at the beach at that moment – to be able to *run to the sea*. And then the U2 song, *One Tree Hill* started playing in my head for the next few hours. I love that song. It reminds me of my college years and brings back so many memories. As a songwriter, I'm often drawn to lyrics of songs. Of course, I had to open my browser and look at the words to *One Tree Hill* on that chilly van ride, and read the incredible story behind it. There were lyrics and phrases in that one song that turned into my new series, *Reigning Hearts* (lyrically, Raining Hearts.) Thus, a new trilogy was born: *Run to the Sea* (Book One), *Stars Fall From The Sky* (Book Two), and *A Sun So Bright* (Book Three.) So thank you, Bono and U2, for the inspiration – new stories behind the lyrics. Yes, there is a method to a writer's madness!

Thank you to my critique partner and one of my best girls, CB Deem for being there from the get-go. Our playlists on our writer's retreats are my favorite. I covet your feedback and suggestions *always*!

To fellow romance author and new friend, Gigi Blume,

I can't even begin to thank you for your marketing expertise and help when I was at my wits end (can you say cover reveal?!) Seriously, you had your own incredible release going on and took precious time to help poor me. I can't wait to hug you in person!

Thank you, Eva Talia, my cover artist at Eva Talia Designs. You nailed it on the first try! Thank you for your patience during my OCD moments of perfection. I can always count on you.

To my editor and friend, Vicky Burkholder for being able to take on this project with hardly any notice. As always, you make me a better writer!

For my author friends, ARC & beta readers – your enthusiasm for my work never goes unnoticed. There really are no words. For all the bloggers associated with Itsy Bitsy and Love2Read Romance, THANK YOU for getting me on the map! I can't imagine a book release without you.

To my family, especially my frat house of boys – I love and adore you with everything I have! Your continued support and belief in me is what keeps me going.

For my readers – you continue to rock my world! The consistent reviews you have posted on Goodreads, BookBub and Amazon are virtual hugs that I cherish.

I sincerely hope you will take this series journey with me into the lives of three very different women. It's gonna be a *blast*!

Stay tuned – and remember, love always wins!

KG
xoxo

ABOUT THE AUTHOR

Dubbed, "The Singing Author," KG Fletcher lives in Atlanta, GA with her husband Ladd and three sons. She is an active member of RWA and Georgia Romance Writers. She was a singer/songwriter in Nashville, TN and a recipient of the "Airplay International Award" for "Best New Artist" showcasing original songs at The Bluebird Café. She earned her BFA in theater at Valdosta State College and has traveled the world professionally as a singer/actress. She currently gets to play rock star as a backup singer in the National Tour, "Remember When Rock Was Young – the Elton John Tribute." www.almosteltonjohn.com

KG is a hopeless romantic continuing her work on her original cabaret act called, "The Novel Romantic – an unexpected evening of sweet & spicy love" to help promote her romance novels. She is also a conference speaker and shares how music can enhance a writer's experience.

Find KG online:

Website: www.kgfletcherauthor.com

Twitter: www.twitter.com/@kgfletcher3

Instagram: www.instagram.com/kellyf9393/

Facebook: www.facebook.com/kgfletcherauthor/

Amazon: www.Amazon.com/author/kgfletcher

Songs/Cabaret: www.kgfletcherauthor.com/songs--cabaret.html

Pinterest: www.pinterest.com/kfletcher3

Goodreads:
https://www.goodreads.com/book/show/43020858-run-to-the-sea

Spotify Playlist: https://goo.gl/jPeKgK

BookBub: https://www.bookbub.com/profile/kg-fletcher

YouTube Channel with book trailers:
http://www.youtube.com/channel/UCxD4r0_mOYWWi VmlT_JSSdg

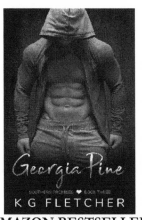

Georgia Pine

SOUTHERN PROMISES ♥ BOOK THREE

K G FLETCHER

(AMAZON BESTSELLER)
Southern Promises ~ Book Three

The agony of defeat never felt so real.

Never in a million years did Jessica Kaufman think she would be divorced from her real-estate mogul husband and left to raise four young daughters on her own in an affluent Atlanta subdivision. The very last thing she expects is an encounter with her gorgeous gardener who looks more like a sexy beast from her daughters' favorite Disney movie. She is smitten with his evergreen eyes, wild mane of hair and impressive stature.

Tim McGill is in hiding – his reputation and celebrated career on the West Coast left in shambles. He moves far away to distance himself from his downfall and inconspicuously tends the upper-class landscapes to keep his renowned identity a secret. Unlike his typical wealthy clients, Jessica doesn't seem to mind that he's a gardener. One spark between them is all it takes to ignite a fiery passion that could explode if Tim's identity is revealed. He must earn Jessica's trust and finally come to terms with what he has lost.

Can Tim open his heart wide enough to let in a beautiful mother and her four little girls? Or will his Southern Belle turn her back on him and walk away from their happily-ever-after?   https://goo.gl/BHgktw

Southern Promises ~ Book Two

First rule in business – never let them see you with your pants down.

Hartford Parker is a disgraced real estate broker hiding out in his sister's condo in suburban Atlanta. Swearing off women after an embarrassing indiscretion at a black-tie event, Hart now indulges in drinking and working out as he tries to come to terms with his unexpected firing at a prestigious DC firm.

Across town in a run-down and forgotten part of the city, Gia Bates is struggling to make ends meet at her failing dance studio. Secretly working part-time as a Marilyn Monroe impersonator for a seedy entertainment company has Gia feeling trapped in her debt while slowly chipping away at her passion and solace in dance.

The handsome playboy and the dancer with legs-for-days find themselves at the same party and end up on an uncertain path full of sex, secrets, and shame. As they move forward in a spicy tango, can the two of them ever dance in sync? Will they fight for their own happily ever after or will Hart be left with nothing more than Georgia on his mind?

https://goo.gl/bK4ttn

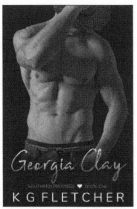

Southern Promises ~ Book One

Everyone in Nashville knows Georgia Clay.

He's the handsome, award-winning songwriter rubbing elbows with the elite stars of country music. An incredible talent in his own right, Clay has always hesitated to step into the spotlight on his own for fear his debilitating childhood secret will rear its ugly head.

Katie Parker is a workaholic Southern beauty who's first love is her career. It's not just her knowledge of the cut-throat insurance business she has skillfully navigated over the years, but her tenacity and gumption in climbing the corporate ladder.

The musician and career woman run into each other in the heat of the Atlanta summer at their ten-year high school reunion and unexpectedly end up in the bed of his pickup truck talking till dawn. As they forge ahead in a passionate long-distance relationship, can Clay admit to Katie she had his heart a long, long time ago? Will her drive and encouragement finally be the reason Georgia Clay takes a chance on his career…and love?

https://goo.gl/WM3MmH

Other books by KG Fletcher

Lounge singer, Lauren Rose lived her comfortable life in Atlanta always dreaming of making it in show biz. When she unexpectedly meets British male super-model, David Randle at a gig at the posh St. Regis Hotel, she is swept away by his striking good looks and lilting cadence.

In town for his sister Catherine's nuptials to NASCAR driver, Brian Brady, David invites Lauren to the wedding on a whim. The two instantly bond over music, fashion and family. They continue their new relationship in New York City when David invites Lauren to see him in action at a high-profile fashion shoot for his debut fragrance, "Drive."

Sparks fly when his assistant, Sabrina Watson is none too happy that his new girlfriend has interrupted his grueling, fast-paced schedule. She becomes fixated on separating the happy couple who are falling in love.

Traversing the East Coast and Europe with the paparazzi in hot pursuit, David and Lauren navigate the precarious path of fame, fashion and fate.

https://www.amazon.com/dp/B073MPWGHS

Her heart searched for a melody. Will the love song she finally hears be loud enough to drown out the screaming memories of her past?

Back-up singer Casey lived the old anthem, "work hard, play harder." When she meets handsome sub-drummer, Sam Wildner on a gig, their attraction is immediate. The two musicians forge ahead in a dizzy rhythm of passion and music, both impressed by each other's harmonious abilities. When Sam learns of Casey's family trauma involving her sister's abusive ex-boyfriend, he commits to being there for her and her young niece who is caught in the middle.

The melody of their love song rings loudly in Casey's ears as she and Sam navigate the precarious fast lane of jealousy, murder and rock 'n roll.

https://www.amazon.com/dp/B06XFVWQR2

unexpected

KG FLETCHER

Recently jilted Josephine Davis wasn't looking for love…. A chance encounter along the sweltering highway with Atlanta's own millionaire bachelor changed all that. Devastatingly handsome and full of unexpected talents, William Prescott Harrington, III shows beautiful Josie a life that she could have only dreamed of; his excessive wealth and generosity eventually threatening her very existence. Two star-crossed lovers from polar opposite sides of Atlanta navigate their way through a maze of greed and jealousy desperate for only one thing – each other.

Her heart made a wish. Will her dream become reality or will the nightmare destroy them all?

https://www.amazon.com/dp/B01LYDLUSD

Thank you for reading!
If you enjoyed my story, please leave a review and tell
your friends!

For the latest upcoming KG Fletcher releases and tour
dates, sign up for my newsletter at:

www.kgfletcherauthor.com/contact.html

COMING SUMMER 2019
Stars Fall From the Sky
(Ginger's story)
Book Two in the Reigning Hearts Series
By KG Fletcher

COMING CHRISTMAS 2019
A Sun So Bright
(Fiona's story)
Book Three in the Reigning Hearts Series
By KG Fletcher

Add to your Goodreads TBR:
https://www.goodreads.com/author/show/16175390.
K G Fletcher

#lovewins

275

Made in the USA
Columbia, SC
08 April 2019